ONE NIGHT IN THE DENSE RAIN FOREST

-Dr. PRERNA SINGLA

Amidst the middle of the dense forest the darkness reigned even in the brightest of the light and the loneliness was over-powering the mind of Trisha when even after a struggle of many days she could not find the way out of the dense forests of Amazon. No one to talk to, not even a single human seen and the ambience of the forest even though appeared very attracting in the beginning but now had started to scare her.

It was not really the fear of the known, but was the fear of unknown, the fear of being stuck at an abandoned place of the planet alone, fear of dying at such a haunting place, fear of so much more that Trisha could not describe in words but feel and cry. Her tears slipped off the margins of her eyes slowly, her voice sobbing in the undertones. What was the use of crying out loud too? No matter how much she cried there was no one to hear her. It was like being trapped in a huge box with green scenery inside. The trees had started to haunt her too. But the weird nature of the Mother Nature, it scares you and also shelters you.

But somehow Trisha kept moving, tired, lost energy, dehydrated but somehow surviving. And then when after 3 days eating the fallen fruits and the leaves of the plants as if grazing like a cow, her body could not get enough nutrition it collapsed to the state of temporary unconsciousness.

It was either a matter of fate or of luck that by the time she was unconscious, no wild animal crossed that section of the forest, not even snakes. But then she in her temporary state of unconsciousness felt that her body is weightless, as if either floating on water or a sack of air. And it was because it was picked by someone of her species.

Still unable to open her eyes, Trisha lay as is. It was only after a few more hours when Trisha opened her eyes in a series of sudden blinks. As she woke up she found herself in a cave, lying on a bed of collected grass with a bonfire warming the cave forming a cosy set up. Nearby lay a mug with some water in it and a satchel.

Trisha looked around if someone was present there wondering who could have rescued her from the proceeding death of loneliness in an abandoned portion of a huge forest, but she found no one. Very thirsty she extended her hands, picked up the mug and greedily drank the water in the mug without even giving a second thought to the possibility of anything dangerous in it. What could have been worse than death anywhere in the world?? She wondered.

Just then a man with huge black boots entered the cave. He wore a well fitting blue jeans and a white shirt and carried lots of wood branches in his hand as well as a bag. 'A faulty fashion' she thought to herself the moment she looked at his attire. His face was still hidden behind the huge bundle of woods. Realising he might not fall; she quickly got up to give him a hand. Her body still ached, but she somehow managed.

"Thank you", He said.

Trisha smiled in response. Words were rarely shared between the two, mostly because Trisha was not so good at talking and the guy would not even start a conversation. The guy one by one took out a few things from his bag that he had collected and among them was a few bottles filled with dirty water. On the pile of woods he quickly arranged a setting to boil the water in the mug in such a manner that he could deduce purified water from the process. The process of condensation and distillation as Trisha had known but she watched him silently thinking how she failed at doing this. She had known this, but still it never crossed her mind that she could collect water from any source and purify it.

Right after that as the mug had the boiling water on one side of the bonfire, the other side he roasted a few fishes one by one that he had caught for the day. They smelled lovely and Trisha was very hungry but she lacked the boldness with which she could demand the food. She had no right on the food, and she sat wondering if the man would be polite enough to offer her some.

And the moment he finished the first fish he gestured her to come forward and enjoy the meal. "I am not an expert cook, but I guess that should do." He said as he handed the stick to Trish on which the dead roasted fish hung.

"Thanks" Trisha replied hesitantly. "Is there anything vegetarian that can be eaten??"

To this he turned to her and replied, "Yes, there is nice vegetarian restaurant around the corner where you can order anything you want."

Eloquently sarcastic remark it was. Trisha felt bad initially but also realised that she was being too demanding as well as selfless at a place where it was difficult to survive and that she must be thankful to the guy for saving her life. Somehow strengthening her heart and ignoring all the thoughts that came to her mind she closed her eyes partially and ate the fish. To her amazement it was really yummy and by the time she finished he handed her another one. Soon she finished the second fish too. She was so hungry that she had eaten almost a kg of flesh.

Her gaze was glued to the guy whose face shined hot red in the light of bonfire as he noshed the flesh. With hair styled in a perfect army cut, she estimated that he might be an army personnel well equipped with knowledge and expertise to live in a forest like that. Who else in the world has so many arrangements made in a cage?

"How did you find me?" Trisha asked.

"I was going that way, saw you, picked you, brought here." He replied in a monotonous tone.

It seemed to her that the guy was generally harsh by nature but otherwise good at heart. His saving her life was a huge debt in itself.

The silence followed for a few more minutes and finally he broke the silence.

"What brings you to forest?" He asked.

"Adventure." She replied with a smile.

"Foolish" he muttered, to which she chose to keep silent. She was no doubt hurt by the harshness of his words but it was no use arguing a stranger who she doesn't even know. Survival was the need of the hour and not the arguments.

"What brings you here?" she asked emphasizing on 'You' but to her dismay her question was returned unanswered. By now she had understood that this was the guy she would never want to stay with. Never ever. But until she is well enough to carry on her own and find a out, she must stick with him and use him to find a way out.

"Can you tell me the way out?" Trisha asked again while he kept busy enjoying his meal and collecting purified water.

"There" he gestured pointing towards the open end of the cave.

'This guy is filled with sarcasm. Dog.' She thought to herself.

Soon after he was done eating, he collected all the remains and added them to the burning bonfire.

5

"Are you mad? What are you doing?" She said with her words more like a revenge for her bruised ego.

"Saving you from Bear hugs." He replied without even bothering to look at her.

Again the insulting sarcasm now had started to make her feel bad and worse because her presence, her beauty had no effect on him. She had met so many guys who had been crazy about her beauty but this guy never even looked at her twice.

'Is he married? Is he gay?' she wondered... thinking to herself, the insecurity had started to get her anxious about her own personality ... "I am not appealing enough?" she thought.

'It has now become a matter of a girl's self respect to be appealing to a guy.' She thought to herself determined to make a mark of her personality on his mind before she could go her way. The entire thing would serve two purposes; she would find her way out and also find a way in his heart only to leave one day soon. She wanted him to feel as bad as she was feeling by his rough behaviour.

Was it bruised ego or over sensitivity?? Even Trish had no clue.

Sitting like a silent stone in a corner of the cave she sat thinking all these things while he started unbuttoning his shirt on the other corner of the cave that caught her gaze. A well sculpted torso with each muscle shining like leather, he was a marvellous piece to look at. Maybe that is why he had big ego.

Songs of passion and hatred rang in her ears as she watching him undress partially. Grave silence the ambience had on its lips, the only noise was the burning of the wood, while the silent passion burnt in her heart.

The moment he turned and and met his gaze to hers, she blinked close her eyes pretending the mannerisms that one must have. He understood, but replied nothing. A strange nervousness he could hear in her long breaths.

"Don't worry; you are safe here, from animals as well as from me. I am not the kind of guy." He said as he seated himself on the bed of grass. She slowly opened her eyes to look at him but said nothing. Where was their silence headed? Was it headed towards being comfortable in each other's presence?? It was probably the first time ever he had talked a little okay.

The glaze of the burning fire shined in her sleepless eyes as she kept looking at her which can be mostly perceive as staring than looking. He in an uncaring manner went off to sleeping on his cosy grass bed and also reflecting that in his mannerisms. A guy would, out of courtesy, offer the best bed to the lady first. The best bed it can be said in a jungle setting, better than sleeping on the rock which Trisha had to that night, but that never offended her. She was now being used to the harshness in his nature. Since after she had woken up, anything she had witnessed about the guy was his harshness and nothing else. Who was he after all and what makes him so harsh? What makes him live in the jungle in a cave in a home setting???

A desperate woman does a better research than a jealous woman", she uttered to herself and quickly in a snap without making noise she fetched the satchel that she had seen that very day. Hopeful of finding some information, she unbuckled the flap of the satchel. Who uses a traditional type of bag in this modern age? Things about this man were highly contradictory. His attire was ultra modern and his ways were extra primitive.

One by one she took out the things from the satchel, herbs, stones, and a pair of clothes, a wind cheater, a knife, and a bottle that looked more like a solid bodied water bottle she used to carry to school when she was a child. No pictures were found, no other information. The exercise was a waste, now the only information she could have was directly from him.

Anyhow, too tired to be very energetic she placed all the things back to the satchel, slowly and silently tiptoed to the grass bed and laid herself right next to him. She knew that a contact to a woman's body can drive any man crazy, that too as beautiful as she was. It was impossible to believe that she had no impact on him.

The morning followed and the cave was much illuminated by the morning day light that woke him up. As he blinked open his eyes he found himself wrapped in the arms of Trisha. The feel of her long fingers and beautiful nails on his bare body had started to initiate strong attraction in him, but at no cost can he cross the line with her. It was not that she was not attractive, but that his mission, his goals would forfeit if fell for the charms of the woman and that could be a trap too. Who knows?

Anyhow he moved out of the bed, and left the cave. The bon fire had also reduced to ashes by then. A few minutes later Trisha also woke up. Not finding him anywhere inside the cave she wondered if he had left, since the satchel was also absent. Guilty that she had committed a mistake, she decided to move out and search for him. It was important for her to search him out if she wanted to find a way out.

Heading out, searching and searching, here and there, she soon reached a waterfall that was more than a serene beauty in a forest and there he was, drenched in the serene inviting waters of the waterfall, having a shower in the natural falls. He could be the most adventurous creature to live with. Silently she peeked from behind the trunk of a tree enjoying the scene and a naughty thought crawled into her mischievous mind. She took the satchel off while camouflaging herself behind the trees and hid it behind the bushes.

And just after that she stepped into the coldest waters she had ever imagined. It just heightened the oxytocin rush into her.

"What are you doing?" he asked annoyed.

"Only freshening up... Under the falling waters.... with you..." she said smiling.

His forehead wrinkled into utter annoyance.

"Don't be mad. Your desperation has controlled the little senses that you somehow have." He said angrily but Trish was still unmoved.

"Yes. You read me right. Now that my desperation is ruling me, let it." Saying she started to unbutton her soggy white shirt through which was shining her sculpt body. And just then a strong wave struck her and she slipped in the waters.

Instantly he reached up for her and held her in his arms. Taking advantage of the time she glued her body to his. It was really getting difficult for him to control himself. He wished he could take her right there right then but a little mistake could land them both in trouble. Holding her like a huge monkey holding its child he moved out of the water but she was still unconscious. Guilty for being so harsh with her, he gently laid her on the boundary of stones. Sceptical if he should give her the Cardio Pulmonary Resuscitation he finally decided to go ahead with it. Gently he met his lips with hers; closing her nostrils he pumped in the breath into her. With each time he did that, it would expel water off her lungs, the manoeuvre followed by thumping her chest to regain breath and heart beats.

One more time and she grabbed him suddenly and passionately kissed him. Flabbergasted he moved away but not to leave, the fire of passion had flamed and they made passionate love right there, under the vast sky by the side of the waterfall. She returned him the satchel and he carried her to his cave where they made love the entire day, entire night to wake up bare, glued together the other day.

There was no fear of the world in that forest, no need for privacy too. She felt happy and her deserted desires seemed to be complete with the adventures of the Jungle. They ate whatever he caught from the waterfall earlier that day. The life seemed beautiful as she lay on the grass bed thinking if she could spend her life with this man, even if in the jungle, it would be like living in the dreamland.

"My name is Paul. I am a common man turned anti-national." He said taking out the pistol from a concealed hole in the cave.

"Anti-National??? What do you mean by anti-national?? Are you a.... "Trisha could not believe her ears; her dreamland was suddenly knocked with horror.

"Terrorist!" He said pointing the gun at her and all the jungle heard was a BANG!

#####

THE LOVE TYRE

- PULKIT MOHAN SINGLA

"Susan! You have a new candidate joining today.", said Mr. Sharma rolling his yoga mats after the yoga session was over. He took from his pocket a white page with a few details scribbled on the same. ***Rohan Kapoor , 28 yrs , 5:00 – 6:00 pm*** it said. Susan read the details out loud in a manner of memorising the same keeping in mind the new candidate who was to join her yoga class that day. It will certainly be a boost to her career as a yoga instructor. 'The more the better' she thought to herself.

Right after the afternoon lunch hour there was a knock on her cabin. "May I come in?", said a velvety voice, to which Susan was compelled to hold all that she was doing and looked up. She was struck by wonder the moment her eyes met his. She had never before seen a guy as handsome as that. The features resembled a sculpture carved out of stone.

"Yes, Please.", she replied instantly controlling the anxiety of her attraction.

The door opened and the young man entered her cabin. He was a man with a face completely opposite to the prettiness of his body. A tall bodied but a plum, overweight personality he carried with a partial confidence as he walked in.

"Hi I am Rohan. I have come for the Yoga classes" He said entering the room.

"Umm! You were going to come at 5 PM." , Susan replied in a half confused tone, still under the effect of his charm.

"Yes. I wonder if my time can be extended? I wish to get in shape soonest possible." He said. There was an air of concern in his tone.

"Don't worry. We can take extra sessions and I will prescribe you a proper diet chart along with exercise schedule.", Susan replied smiling.

"You can start from today itself." , she continued.

"Okay" Rohan answered and smiling he got up to take his yoga mat.

While he was away the impatient eyes of Susan were glued to his activities. 'It is a woman's sixth sense that is on the work' they say. She was observing him, his interactions, his actions, everything. It is not that she had a liking for over weight men, but Rohan had a charm none other had till date.

The very first session she dedicated all her time onto setting Rohan's Yogaasana right. Their compatibility seemed to gel.

"Rohan you have to repeat these aasana daily. It will be best if you can shift your time to early morning." She explained after the first session.

"Here is thediet chart I am giving you and you have to follow this. Try to incorporate most of beans in your diet and you will lose fast with the right approach. You will also have to avoid all the oily stuffs and no soft or hard drinks." Susan continued in a tone that sounded not so professional this time which was unlikely of her nature. Never before had this happened that she had mixed her professional and personal life, specially never after her divorce, but this time she was being attracted to Rohan like a magnet and her senses told her that he was equally attracted. But the question of advancing to this extent on the very first day sounds more like a desperation.

"Ohh you are only infatuated towards him since you haven't had a man since ages.", explained her best friend Marie who she met that very evening. Marie was not only her best friend but also like her sister, her advisor in all avenues of life.

"Give it some time. First make sure that the guy is not fraud, only then proceed. You never know how much of a dog a guy can be." Marie suggested.

"Don't worry. I will first satisfy myself only then will proceed. I say you also join the yoga class. I will enrol you without any charge. I want your help with this. If he is a good guy then he might be the best choice." Susan said with a desperation in her words. With such a pleading tone Marie already told that Rohan had blinded her right in the first meet. Now was the time to test this guy. This is how the gang of girls work.

Next day arrived and it came to Susan as a shock when Rohan showed up right at 5AM.

"Ohh! You?? So early?", Stuck with surprise Susan stammered.

"Yes." Rohan replied smiling

"You asked me to shift my time and so I shifted."

Susan had no reply to his sweet answer. She simply smiled and asked him to reach the Yoga hall

As rohan left Susan's cabin, she quickly dialled to Marie.

Ring ring.... ring ring.... ring ring... The number you are trying to contact is not answering at the moment.

Ring ring.... ring ring.... ring ring... The number you are trying to contact is not answering at the moment.

Maarie was probably sleeping at that time. Low hearted and very much nervous she quickly sent a text to Marie and proceeded to the Yoga hall.

'The last time she re-read the text. "Marie, this guy has arrived right in the first class just as I asked him to. I am both nervous and excited. What do I do? You join me soonest you can.'

The session started and as she went near Rohan to correct his posture, sweet fragrance filled her senses. She was being lead towards him in such an uncontrolled manner that it seemed to be destined.

After about half an hour marie appeared. "Hi. Sorry I got late." She said smiling sheepishly.

"It's okay Marie. Glad you joined us." Susan replied in the same professional tone even to Marie but she gestured through her eyes pointing towards Rohan.

Marie quickly took seat and soon after the first session was over she initiated informal introduction to all the members who enrolled to the group. Trick was to initiate contact with Rohan so that she can know him better. Once known she wil be able to test him better.

"Hi. I am Marie. Your co-yoga mate." Married said extending her hand for a formal handshake.

"Hi I am Rohan. Nice to meet you Yoga mate." Rohan replied smiling and Marie smiled in response.

"So? You come here everyday?" Marie asked boldly while Susan observed their conversation from the corner pretending that she doesn't know Marie.

"Umm.. I joined yesterday. How about you?" Rohan replied and counter questioned,

"I was a regular member here, but discontinued in between due to work and all. Now joined back from today. It is like I am jumping in and out.. hehe." Marie replied laughing

"It is good. I should also learn for your schedule and try and stay regular." Rohan replied.

"What do you do?", Marie quickly asked before the conversation died.

"I am a lawyer." Rohan replied.

"Wow! That is great. Lawyers are liears." Marie replied laughing.

"Haha! Consequences of the profession." Rohan replied reciprocating the laughter.

"Ok Mr. Lawyer, It is really nice to meet you. Let us catch up for a cup of coffee some evening? My woman instinct tells me that you are very interesting to talk to." Marie said.

"Sure. Anytime you say." Rohan replied humbly.

The took took their ways. Rohan checked out from the yoga hall and Marie went to Susan's cabin. Soon susan followed to the cabin.

"Yaar! Teri toh nikal padi." Marie said in utter excitement.

"He is a laywer and very nice to talk to. I have made friends with him and asked him out for a coffee. Abb tu dekhna, how I test him. Although he seems like a good guy." Marie continued in a stretch.

"Thank youuuu.." Susan shouted in excitement hugging Marie tightly.

"Now give me his number." Marie asked.

"Number??" Susan replied flabbergasted.

"Haan re. Check the register. All the members who enrol have to add their mobile numbers.

Nodding in affirmation Susan took the register out from the office, searched out Rohan's name and saved his contact as well as gave the number to marie.

The evening followed. Rohan as usual was spending his quality time on the Balcony of his beach side house. And just then his phone rang.... The ringtone sung the hyms of Titanic.

'Hello." , he said

"Hello. How are you?" Asked the sweet voice of a lady. The voice was unfamiliar to Rohan

"Who are you?" Rohan asked.

"You forgot so quickly? I am your ex." , She replied in a demanding tone.

"Are you sure? You don't sound like her." Rohan argued.

"Yes Mister. I am more than sure. My voice got a little sore and you forgot me???" The voice counter argued.

"Okay my apologies Tina. I believe you. But tell me, how did you come back from heaven??" Rohan asked with a tone of seriousness.

To such a witty question Marie was speechless but was intrigued by the replies of Rohan.

Laughing she said. "You are a hard nut to crack Rohan."

"I know Marie." Rohan replied laughing

"Hey! How did you know that It's me????" Marie enquired.

"You see I am a lawyer." Rohan said smugly

"Still! Tell ya." Marie insisted

"Nopes. That's a secret. You take that I am like Sherlok Holmes. Nothing is hidden from me." Rohan replied and smartly escaped answering to her.

"Ok tell me are you free tomorrow? There is a Book fare in the Town. Let's catch up if you can spare some time." Marie asked. Their compatibility seemed to flow naturally. It felt as if Marie had known him since ages. But she was careful not to fall for Rohan since her best friend was head over heels for Rohan and she did not wish to ruin any relationships.

"Yes sure" Rohan replied as Marie had so many things going on in her mind. He seemed so good. How was it possible that he was still single? Or maybe he had some past? Don't know, but the things have to be known before proceeding further. After all it was the question of Susan's life and Marie did not want her to repeat the mistake she did with David who Susan had divorced due to increasing domestic violence by him. David also seemed like a great guy in the beginning, but his true face came into the light only later. But anyways, let us test this guy.

"Okay. See ya." Marie said and hung the phone instantly. She was working all the tricks a woman should, to lure a man. This was the very first test Rohan had to pass if he has to reach Susan. It all sounded stupid, since they did not even know if Rohan liked Susan or not. So much of fatigue only for Susan and her one sided liking.

Right after the conversation was over Marie turned to Susan who had been impatiently sitting right beside her and hearing their conversation as the speaker of the mobile was on.

"So we are meeting tomorrow. Yippieee!!" maria said rejoicing.

"But why you didn't mention that I will be coming along?" Susan enquired.

"So that he is caught by surprise. You will enter the scene 15 minutes after I meet Rohan. I want to see his reaction and at the same time our trick should not be obvious on him.

"great." Susan answered.

The day passed and another day appeared. Yoga class in the morning went well. As usual Marie seated herself beside Rohan and Susan was keeping in touch with the conversation briefly. Marie had warned her to not to look desperate.

For Susan the day passed with excitement of the evening. She spent all her day trying out dresses and getting ready in the best of the ways. Although divorced but she looked like a young princess.

Finally the hour of their meeting arrived. As decided, Marie and Rohan went together in Rohan's car. The tickets were booked and the both enjoyed the literary ambience sorting through the books that were exhibited in the Book fair. It had been some time and they stopped at the coffee corner to spend some time having coffee.

"Rohan, I want to say something." Marie said in a tone of hesitation.

"Yes?" Rohan replied with a tone of convern.

"You are a nice guy Rohan. I like you... as a person... as a friend." Marie said in a hesitatnt manner inidicative of her interest in him.

"Thank you I respect your feelings but I hope that you do not develop any more feelings for me, since I have started to like some other girl and will not be able to reciprocate the same feelings to you. But yes of course we can always remain friends." Rohan replied gently.

"Hmm... Okay. If you do not mind, can I ask who is that girl??" Marie asked the question whose answer she always wanted to find out. It was very important to know if Rohan is dating someone before Susan could attach feelings for him. Else, it would turn out to be an unnecessary heartache.

"Please keep it to yourself. I am sharing with you in complete faith." Rohan muttered

"Absolutely." Maria replied.

"It's Susan. I do not know if she likes me but I have started to develop a liking for her. She is absolutely my kind of girl, gentle, intelligent, beautiful, and a person with a beautiful heart. " Rohan said with eyes radiating excitement.

Yes.... that is what Marie wanted to find out. She sat there unable to hold up excitement and trying to pretend how normal the news is for her. A few minutes later Susan appeared, as decided by Marie.

It was after that the things took up a speedy course. Marie explained everything to Susan and also assured that he is the type of guy who will never betray her. Rohan came out to be among the dreams guys Susan had dreamt to live with. A guy who was humble, who was caring, even though he was overweight but the beauty his soul held was above all prettiness in the world.

Soon Rohan proposed Susan and she accepted. Being self dependent and from a liberal family, he faced no issues from his parents. Susan's parents were happy that she was going to settle down once again. The marriage was arranged in both Indian setting as well as in the Church.

The day arrived. Susan looked like a princess in white attire. The couple had written their own vows of togetherness and the very evening the marriage took place in the Indian setting. The red zardozi saree draped elegantly around her looked like a traditional Indian beauty. The day marked the most important day in their life and also marked the beginning of love and happiness in Susan's life

... *And they lived happily ever after....*

#####

A Kind Of Cancer, Depression

- Aseer

He never knew that another world existed outside his dark room where he stayed all alone. His clothes were dirty like he hadn't changed them in years. Some motivational and philosophical books were his sole companions along with few pieces of sharp blades and an unused first aid box.

He was unusually quiet, not even talking to himself. He used his cell phone to access the internet and Google some facts about depression. He never called anyone or answered any phone calls except his mother's. He had become the slave of his loneliness because he had forgotten to speak for himself.

More often than not people who never speak for themselves or are interrupted midway while trying to do so go into a state of mind where they think, they are useless and even their words make no difference in anyone's life leave alone their existence. The feeling of being called useless or a loser blocks your mind, pushing you to a zone of loneliness which slowly metamorphoses into to a world known as depression. This was the same phase which Arnab was going through.

He took hold of a blade with his left hand and moved it towards his right hand where a lot of scars were staring back at him. Every time he ran the blade over his hand and made the cut, he experienced immense joy of hurting himself. No, he wasn't suicidal. Killing himself was never an option, all he wanted to do was to hurt himself. It helped him check his endurance of pain, of how much he can suffer in his life and also helped him forget the other pain of life, of living.

When he had made his first cut, he had cried like anything. It had become a ritual for him now, crying and shouting alone had become his daily routine, but after sometime he had given up crying as he had given up many other things like wandering aimlessly, eating regularly and taking shower. The wounds and scars on his body no longer hurt him. He didn't feel any pain now whenever he made a cut but derived some sense of pleasure from it.

Without a fraction of a thought he positioned the sharp blade on his hand and pressed it, with the right amount of pressure; strong enough to let it bleed and subtle enough to not cause more damage leading to death. All of a sudden he saw his mother's name flashing on his mobile screen. He stopped himself midway to answer the phone.

"Hello Mom!" He smiled...

He didn't forget to pretend. He loved his mom from the core of his heart and this was the only reason he never tried to commit suicide. He knew his mother would never be able to recover if she heard about his death and if she got to know about his situation, how depressed he was then it would hurt her as much as his death. But he was helpless; he had to stay strong in front of her. He never told his mother about his condition. He always smiled while talking to her on the phone so that she wouldn't get any clue about the pain he is going through.

"Are you alright Arnab?" She asked breathlessly.

"Yeah mom, I'm fine. What happened, why are you sounding so tensed?" He could sense the concern in her voice.

"Nothing. I just don't know why I was not feeling good, so I called you." She said in a low tune.

"I love you mom. And relax, I am fine." He tried assuring her.

"I love you too Arnab." She answered.

"Okay now bye, I've got some work to do." He said, fooling her.

"Bye, take care." She replied and disconnected the call.

He thought his mother didn't know anything about his situation but he was wrong. She knew everything about Arnab and what he told on the call was not what he felt like. She could feel his pain, but she never said anything. She knew that Arnab will never do anything wrong and she also knew that he is strong enough to fight any problem. Somewhere she was right but not exactly. Arnab was fighting only to keep himself alive for his mother. He had given up on himself long ago.

Arnab took the blade making a cut on his hand once again with no expression on his face. As if nothing was amiss he casually picked up a motivational book from his shelf and started reading it.

Arnab always read a book after hurting himself. Blood kept dripping out of his hand but he never cared. Whenever he saw blood dripping out of his hand, he felt pleasure and smiled. The blood that dripped out was the only reason which made him smile. He read books which kept him alive along with the cuts. First he made the cuts and then he gained the strength to fight with pain through books and some bookmarks saved in his phone named as motivational quotes. Arnab read books from the motivational genre to stay alive, hanging dangerously somewhere between life and death. He never wished to completely surrender himself to any of these be it life or be it death.

"Who are you?" Arnab asked the man sitting in the dark.

"Someone whom you always ignored!" came the reply

"It means that I don't want to talk to you, whosoever you are. So why are you here? "Arnab asked.

"I am here to take you to the world full of happiness." The man answered.

Before he could say anything the man asked a question to Arnab.

"Why do you feel alone?"

"What type of a question is it? I am alone that's why I feel alone. My father doesn't love me. For him I am just an unwanted waste whose place is there in the dustbin. I am 25 and I'm unable to earn a single penny. Whatever work I started, it always failed giving me nothing. I let down my father at every step. According to him I can never give happiness to anyone because I am useless and a loser. I am an insensitive guy who never feels the pain of his father. I kept doing whatever I loved to and I always failed. I am unable to take the right decision in my life which again shows that I'm failure. Even after walking on my selected path against my father I am unable to keep myself happy, which shows I'm a useless creature on this earth that has no feelings for anyone, not even for himself." Arnab said in frustration, venting out all the bottled emotions till now

"So you call yourself a loser?" The man asked.

"Yes!" Arnab answered.

"Everybody is." He stated as a matter of fact.

"How?" Arnab asked.

"We all are born by the same process. No one in this world has any kind of magical power with him. We are all the same. Winning and losing are two sides of the same coin. If you've achieved something and

you take it as an achievement than you are winner, but if you don't take it as an achievement then you'll always take yourself as a loser. Similarly, not everything what you achieved is an achievement for others, for them it may be nothing. We can never decide that we are winners or losers. It's always decided by the people who are around us. So keep up the good work till your last breath. Don't think about winning or losing. Just keep one thing in your mind that when you die, people will call your name with respect and this will be the biggest achievement for you and that respect will be your winning trophy. People never respect you while your struggle and life is full of struggles till death." The man answered confidently.

"How can I think in such a way when I have no emotions left in me?" Arnab was not convinced by his answer so he asked the man.

"You are filled with emotions. Your love towards your mother proves that." The man seemed to smile now.

"Wait a minute, how do you know about this?" Arnab asked in a tone that reflected shock.

"I told you that I am the one whom you always ignored. I know everything about you." The man replied and continued, *"Just because you don't feel any pain when you cut yourself or don't smile doesn't mean you have no emotions left. If you can feel yourself when you're hurt then you are not emotionless. People around you don't love you because you don't love yourself. If you don't love yourself then never expect anyone to love you. People never waste their time on dead things until and unless it doesn't have any charm."*

Arnab was impressed by his answer but not fully satisfied, so he asked. **"What about loneliness which I feel even when I've people around me?"**

"You always love to dominate yourself and when you find that you are unable to do the same you feel that no one listens to you or no one is respecting your views. Instead of saying anything listen to them carefully, don't utter a single word until they don't ask you to say. Your words are so precious that they don't deserve to be wasted on someone who doesn't want to listen to you. You never try to speak; you always try to dominate that's why people never listen to you. This is the reason you feel alone everywhere. Just speak instead of dominating and feel the love of the people around you." The man answered.

Arnab knew he was dominating was and that convinced him about the answer but he wanted to know the real reason behind the fact why he was not able to come out of depression. So he again asked a question. **"Why I am not getting out from depression?"**

"Like cancer, depression is also a disease; a disease which never gets cured easily. But it doesn't mean that it cannot be cured. Cancer breaks people mentally and so does depression. Let's talk about cancer only. When people come to know that they are suffering from cancer they automatically move to the state of mind where they think they are going to die very soon. But some people still stay positive and live the life as they were living before they came to know about that disease. This positive feeling helps them to fight with cancer and it also plays a very important role in curing it. I accept it is not a surety that those positive feelings will defiantly cure cancer but it is sure that these feelings never

stop you from living." The man said answering Arnab's question and continued, "*When it comes to depression it is same as cancer. You move to the depression zone where you find nothing is happening according to you. You find yourself alone, you cry, you hurt yourself, you begin to think about ending your life. You keep yourself alone but never think about yourself that's why you hurt yourself every moment. All the negativity around you embraces you when you stop thinking about yourself. Instead of keeping yourself alone try to face the world of those demons which is killing you from inside. When you face them, angels inside you awake automatically and give you power to fight with demons. Those angels are none other than your positive energy.*"And saying this, the man disappeared.

When Arnab woke up he had a smile on his face. It was something which had happened after a long span of time. Arnab searched for the man here and there but he found him nowhere that's when he realized that he was dreaming that man who knows everything about him was none other than his own soul.

His smiling face was a sign to himself that his soul wanted him to move on towards the path of positivity. He cleaned his room and then went to take a shower. The angels inside him were now trying to wake up slowly.

He called his mother. She was very happy that Arnab himself had called her, something she had been waiting for him to do since ages. She could now feel the charm in his voice and sense the positive vibes. While talking with his mother, Arnab felt that she knew everything what he had been trying to hide from her. She started crying and disconnected the call saying *"I love you Arnab."*

Arnab started crying after the call ended, but this time with a smile. His depression was cured by the angels. He then started a new journey which was full of positive vibes and without the fear of becoming a loser.

#####

Porch Swing

Anshuma Sharma

She knew she'd never forget that memory even if she tried to. It was burnt in her mind; the imprint, so strong that it'd never go away. She remembered watching them once, from her window, wondering why they weren't speaking; her seven year old mind wondering if mommy and daddy had a fight. But then her fears were put to rest, she saw their hands intertwined while they sat on the porch swing; although they were still not speaking. She hadn't thought of that memory until she was much, much older. Until she met him.

He was charming, made her laugh, bought her the odd little trinkets that had the most special memories attached to them, taught her how to love. And oh, she was madly in love with him.

He was her first thought every day, the one person whose mere presence made her smile giddily. If there was anything she was sure of, it was him. They'd make it. He was her everything. Harsha had been wildly in love with Abhay. He'd given her all she had ever asked for and so much more. And that's when it had come up. The porch swing. She hadn't realized the full implication of what she'd seen. She wanted that. That peace, that tranquility, that absolute surety about the one you love. And all through her adult life she'd sworn that the day she'd find someone with whom she could sit on the swing while holding hands and not say anything for the better part of their time without feeling restless, he'd be the one. And she'd done that. With Abhay.

It was pouring, the rain cascading in rivulets everywhere. The garden was drenched and the sound of pouring rain slashed through her conscious as she tried to blink back the tears.

Why wouldn't he understand? It was all fine till now then why was he being so stubborn? His question hung in the air, shrouding the two of them. It was too much, too soon. Her chest constricted, the breaths coming in shallow gasps; no one had told her it'd be like this. No one had told her it could be so excruciatingly painful that she wouldn't be able to breathe .

She was supposed to be over him. Over Abhay, over every memory of his. And she was trying but it was too damn hard.

She looked sideways, his gaze had never left hers. Why was he doing this? She tried to tell him, she wasn't ready, she wasn't ready to do this just yet but he was unrelenting, his stare never wavered. She saw his conflict in his stormy gray eyes; she hated that they were gray, they were always blue when he smiled.

She pleaded, one last time.

"Please…Himanshu. Please."

His turmoil came through when his voice cracked. "I can't do this anymore Harsha. I can't compete with him anymore, it's too much."

She was hanging on to the last threads of her reserve and they weren't strong enough. "You don't have to compete, Himanshu!"

His eyes flashed at her and her heart squeezed painfully. "Oh but I do, Harsha! He's there in every thought, every action of yours and everytime I do something I hope that someday, you'll learn to love me like you loved him. I don't want that anymore!"

"Himanshu, I love you."

She saw his eyes close briefly and for a moment she hoped he would let go of this topic but a second later he opened them and there was nothing but steely resolve. She took a deep breath, shuddering.

"I know you do, Harsha-"

"Then why-"

"Let me finish. I know you do, but we can't keep doing this, I can't keep doing this. I don't deserve this and neither do you."

"Abhay was-"

She saw his control snap. "Abhay is dead Harsha!"

His voice ricocheted all around her, breaking, tearing, snapping the threads of her reserve as she took in his words. Hot tears escaped her eyes, running ceaselessly down her cheeks as her temper flared. She stood up, wanting to burn this frustration out of her. The rain drenched her in no time and she ran a hand through her hair, anger dripping from her every bone. She looked at him on the swing, his posture rigid with barely suppressed irritation.

"You think I don't know that?! You think I live in this false world where I pretend everything is alright? Well, I don't, Himanshu! I live with it everyday. I live with the fact every fucking day that he and I were in the same car and I out-lived him. So don't tell me he's dead, because I know it better than anyone!"

"Then let go, Harsha! For God's sake, you said you were ready to date again and here we are. I thought you'd moved on!"

She listened to his brazen words; they cut right through her, twisting her insides like someone had plunged a knife through them. She knew they were too far gone to steer clear of this topic now. It would either be resolved, or not."I'm trying, dammit! You think it's easy getting over a dead fiancé? I can't do it overnight!"

"It's been seven years! Seven years since he died and three since we started dating! So don't tell me that I'm being unfair!"

His words stunned her into silence and they both stood there, the rain pouring down on them, his words circling her mind. Seven years. Seven years had passed since he died.

The fact astounded her, knocked the breath out of her lungs and defeated, she sat down on the wet grass her body wet and limp with exhaustion. Why had she held on for so long?

Why was she still holding on? Her mind spun with the realization that he was right. They couldn't do it anymore. She had to stop this because she was hurting him too. She tried to look for it, the missing piece that would compel her to move on. Because she wanted to; move on, that is. And she loved Himanshu, she just needed a way to let go of Abhay. To stop that guilt from choking her, everytime she let herself be happy with Himanshu. She hated the guilt; it always plagued her; like she never deserved to be happy. But she was done.

Done fighting with him, fighting with herself.

She vaguely felt him lead her to the swing and he sat beside her. She could see how tired he was and it hurt her that she was the reason.

His voice was softer when he spoke again, the weariness seeping through it. "I'm not a heartless bastard Harsha. I'm not telling you to forget him, I know you can't. All I'm asking is that are you willing, Harsha? Willing to try to let go? A try is all I'm asking for, if at the end of it, you can't then I'll leave."

"You can't leave." She whispered her anguish coming through. Not again. She hugged her knees closer and heaved a deep breath. She wanted to cry, scream, beat someone up; she didn't know what she was supposed to do. She looked at him, his eyes were closer to blue now but they were adamant. A shudder ripped through her as the wind blew on her wet form.

The sudden silence was overwhelming, it wasn't raining anymore. She saw slivers of sunlight peep through the clouds, making their way towards them, weak at first but shining brighter as they moved. She thought about all the time they'd spent together. Every memory no matter how insignificant passed through her mind and at the end of it she knew she couldn't give him up. She loved him. In that moment something shifted in her, she finally understood. She couldn't hold on to Abhay forever, he was her past. But Himanshu was her present and her future too, if she let him in, and she wasn't going to ruin it.

She saw him looking ahead and tapped him on the shoulder. He looked at her and she saw his eyes shine with hope and she smiled faintly. If he loved her so much, maybe letting go wasn't that bad an idea. He'd help her with it.

"Himanshu"

His voice was hoarse when he replied. "Yes?"

"I promise to try and let go."

"Will you be my Valentine FOREVER.?

Forever... I promise" He replied and the warmth in his eyes said everything and she locked her fingers with his as she looked ahead, wondering about the endless possibilities in store for them.

For the longest time they sat there the sunlight drying them. She never said a word; she could already feel herself let go of him, bit by bit. If she'd known before that letting go could feel so good, she'd have done it earlier. The hinges of the swing creaked as it rocked gently and she remembered her parents   as   his   thumb   drew   circles   on   her   palm.

Fate

- Tulika Mukerjee Saha

Aditya Roy, Adi to his friends, was a small town boy. He was living his dream at the University of Auckland, New Zealand. His luck had changed suddenly as he was admitted to the University. He had always wanted to become an architect. A foreign degree would equip him with making buildings environment friendly. Today, as the sun rose on the Winter Auckland sky, Adi walked energetically towards the tram station

It had not been all smooth sailing. He had been rejected by the University at first. Then out of the blue, a mail informed him of his admission as a place had fallen vacant. He recalled how he had jumped at the opportunity and payedobeisance to a variety of Gods. Adi fell into the into the rhythm of classes, canteen, tram and Charlotte's. where he was renting a room.. Adi found that the 'History of architecture' class brought mundane pillars and arches a kind of excitement which reminded him of India in all its variety. Adi now felt that there was a mystery to unravel in each building, a portal to the past in every doorway and a window to the people who lived there.

After classes, Adi was called to the admissions office. The paperwork for the transfer of admission from the previous student to himself had some loop holes.

Adi sat down and filled up the required forms patiently. While at the counter, Adi, wondered what may have caused the student to withdraw.

"Why did the student withdraw?" he asked curiously.

"Oh! The previous one. Why do you want to know?"

"Just curious."

The admissions clerk looked down at the paper in her hand and froze for a second.

She looked at Adi. "Are you certain?"

 "Yeah, go ahead."

"It says here 'sudden demise' ." Her voice becomes soft. Adi stands still for a moment.

Could it be? He takes a deep breath and asks. "What was his name?"

"Alex, Alex Calvin Samuel. He was from your country, India you know."

Adi's face had become ashen.

"Did you know him?" enquired the kind lady.

"No.....no ....yes ....I mean ...in passing."

"I am so sorry."

Adi's walked with leaden feet to the tram stop. He hoped Charlotte would be at home. He needed to share this.

He entered the house. Charlotte emerged from the study in a pair of loose trousers and a loose fitting shirt.

"Cough up young man! What's eating you?"

Adi clears his throat and begins as soon they are settled comfortably.

"Do you know Charlotte that there is a clock at every railway station in India?

I was waiting in front of that clock for the bus to my connecting flight from Bombay to Melbourne. It showed 11 AM. My family had thoughtfully packed a variety of essentials into two very large bags which I was struggling with the as the bus arrived.

I heard a deep voice say,' Let me help you.'

'Hi I am Alex, Alex Calvin Samuel' said the deep voice, seating itself beside me. I turned to thank him and noticed that his dark, angular face with startling deep set blue eyes. Alex was lean and tall, not unusual for one from the south of India. He was dressed in casuals. He sat stone still after that.

Suddenly, he seemed to come alive. He pointed to a clock on a passing cafe and said, 'It is 12:00 PM. Do you see that cafe?' He continued without waiting for my response. 'There was a rather strange occurrence here. A young man was found dead.' The traffic had caused the bus to come to a standstill about five hundred meters from the cafe.

41

'See you can still see the blood stains,' pointing to darkened red stains on the cafe glass, being scrubbed by a cleaner. I remember I had laughed nonchalantly and said that it looked more like paint.

Alex smiled and continued as it I had said nothing ' The fellow had just reached Bombay in search of a job from Kerala. No relatives, no friends. He'd gone to the cafe for ...coffee.' The bus crawled forward through the midday traffic. I yawned inwardly, but there was no stopping Alex. 'The fellow had had a huge fight with his father. He'd eloped with a Hindu girl.'

Adi cleared his throat. 'So where was I ...yes.... Alex continued... his father, and some hoodlums from the village chased after him. He ran for his life. Savitri joined him at the appointed spot. Savitri, just 16, was excited. It fit her young romantic dreams perfectly. No sooner did she hand her small bundle over to him than the mob, led by his father, reached the house . They ran for their lives.

They entered a warehouse, full sacks of grain and buried themselves in separate sacks. The mob soon barged into the warehouse. Terrible screams filled the room as they hacked at the jute sacks. They drew out the unconscious couple from their respective sacks."

"That sounds terrible. Were they badly hurt?" Charlotte enquired.

"Luckily the boy was unhurt except for a few cuts over his body. Savitri was not so lucky however. She had been stabbed through her heart. The girl's family now were thirsting for his blood. So the boy fled and took the local train to Bombay. He reached Bombay and soon enough Savitri's relatives caught up with him. He was killed a month or so before I left India."

"I understand, it must be upsetting to hear of such vengefulness. But I don't see how this could concern you?" said Charlotte.

"I am coming to that. Alex got off at the next stop. Once I had boarded the aircraft, I settled down to read the paper. In a small corner of the front page was a picture of the boy who had been killed. His face was dark and angular and looked terribly familiar. "

"So you were conversing with a spirit! Pretty upsetting, but Adi it is in the past now isn't it? Charlotte said hopefully taken aback by Adi's expression.

"Charlotte, today the admissions office called me to complete some formalities. You know that the fellow who was to join had backed out. The form said 'sudden demise'.

Charlotte let out a gasp, then quickly recovered. "That may be a coincidence. What was his name?"

"Alex, Alex Calvin Samuel."

A chill settled on the two. The silence in the room was deafening, interrupted only by the chiming of the clock which struck 12.

#####

The Unbeaten

... Journey of an unconditional love

- Jyotirmoy Sarkar

Today my friend has left me, my friendship with Akash is from last twelve years, he is a very decent guy, very calm and quiet, twelve years ago he joined our office and gradually we became friend. I am the only man who became very close to him. He does not have the habit to talk much, he does not have the habit to make huge friends but he is very much helpful and has a very kind heart, whenever any one of our colleague faced any problem, Akash was always there beside them. He is very much reluctant to go for tour, in last twelve years he has left the city maximum for six times. Twenty days ago after going office I saw Akash was absent, I called him but his mobile was switched off, probably he has gone somewhere. I decided to contact him the next day. But in the next day I got neither neither he over phone nor was he in his home. I have seen his sudden disappearance many times but those were for few hours but this time fifteen days has been passed It seemed to me that he is just missing, I was very much worried, there were very few places where he used to go but I did not get him even in those places. Suddenly after twenty days of his disappearance, in an early morning he called me over phone and requested to meet him immediately, when I reached his house a middle aged boy opened the door, first time I am seeing the boy because Akash has kept one maid servant and that person is an aged one. Akash was lying in the bed, I asked him about his health, he said he is totally fine. Things were not at all normal, because Akash is not unsocial, he never behaved in this manner with me, he was lying in the bed closing his eyes and neither he got up nor opened the eyes to well come me. He started to talk---- don't ask where I went, I will tell you everything, first tell me how you are and how your family members are.

I said---- everything is fine

Then he asked about our colleagues and we talked for one hour, Akash was lying in the bed in the same manner, we talked a lot and he was saying various types of jokes and was saying lots of funny incidents, he was very happy, this is the first time in last twelve years I saw him so happy. After lots of talks he told---I have three earnest requests to you, please help me and please don't ask any question now, you will get all answers before today night and you have to stay with me today.

I asked ---what are your requests.

---there is an envelope in the table, that is my resignation letter ,please give it to the head of my office and please book a ticket in train, I have written the booking details in a paper ,you can find it in the table. Then he became silent.

I asked ----what is your third request?

---I will tell you about that in the afternoon.

After spending some time with him I went to do the works and also informed my wife that Akash is back and today I will stay with him. I returned to Akash at 12 pm, he has taken his lunch without me; it was very much strange behavior. I meet him after taking bath and lunch; he was lying in the bed in the same way. I sat beside him.

He started to speak--- I am leaving this city tomorrow forever; I know you have lots of questions in your mind. Why I did not contact with you for so many days? Why I am resigning from job? Etc. ok, I am giving you some of my diaries, you read it then we will talk again in the evening.

I took the diaries and started to read, it took four hours to read the diaries and when my reading was complete I became so much stunned that I became speechless, it took thirty minutes and four peg of whisky to be little normal, it became evening and Akash was sitting in the drawing room, when I entered Akash said--- hope you have got answers of all your questions, this is our last meeting here but remembers whenever you want you can meet me in my village; actually I am heartily inviting you to come to my village with your family.

We spent the whole evening discussing various topics, Akash was very happy, this is the first time I am seeing him to make so many jokes. We took dinner together and went to sleep. The train was scheduled in the early morning, Akash became ready much earlier than me, I know last night he did not sleep, because probably this is the end of a journey, the journey which actually was the reason why Akash is alive, the journey in which Akash would never get peace at the end but still he was walking for someone, except me nobody knows why Akash was walking, his journey was his destination, the destination was walking that's why Akash was walking.

I went to see off my best friend, when he was entering the couch he met a collision with a Lady, she replied angrily and went away. When the train started, I could not resist myself to ask him---do you know who that lady was?

Akash replied--- yes,

I will never forget this painful voice. My best friend left me, it took four days for me to overcome the pain I felt for Akash and from his diaries, in short I am writing what was written on those diaries....

Akash Fallen in love with Ankhi when he was in class eleven standard, they both took admission in same high school, from the childhood Akash is very shy type , he had very few numbers of friend because he was not comfortable to make friends and so it was impossible for him that he could make friendship with Ankhi. The time was going on and Akash's love for Ankhi was increased day by day. Ankhi is very good Girl, among those six diaries one is full with the description of Ankhi. After completing school they took admission in different colleges in the same city, their subjects were different that's why regular meeting with Ankhi became very tough but Akash found out some ways to see Ankhi at least once a day. At that time period, once Ankhi faced a problem, Akash helped her to come out of the problem without informing her, which was the beginning, from that time to till now Akash is helping Ankhi whenever she has faced any problem. After completing master degree Akash was trying for job, he got a job quickly, his financial condition was not good, he has struggled a lot against the problems he has faced in his life but he never forgot Ankhi. Ankhi got married after one year of completing graduation, Akash used to keep information about Ankhi, when he came to know that Ankhi lives in this city, he managed to get a job here so that he can be in touch with Ankhi.

Ankhi has a daughter, she is13 years old, Akash has kept information about Ankhi and her family members, during their bad days Akash has done everything which were in his limit, they never came to know who helps them, I think probably they have thanked God for the help and support.

There was a recent photo of Ankhi and her family members in a diary and also their address, those were for me, Akash has requested me to keep information about Ankhi and if I come to know about any problem in Ankhi's life then I immediately inform him, though he has managed another way to keep info about Ankhi.

Few days ago Ankhi met an accident in which she has lost her both eyes, Akash came to know about it, Ankhi's financial condition is not good at all, Ankhi was planning to live her life with one eye for which her husband has managed to gather money, but it was not a pleasant news for Akash, somehow he managed to donate his both eyes without informing Ankhi and her family members, that's why Akash was absent for few days. I asked Akash ---"why both eyes?"

Akash said---"let her live life with completeness, I have never given her any partial things, I have dedicated my whole life for her then why not the both eyes?"

Ankhi will never come to know that....Those are the eyes which always used to look for her, whenever Ankhi will look herself in mirror her eyes will be very happy because those are the eyes which used to find Ankhi madly, those are the eyes which never became tired to stare at the picture of Ankhi, sometime for whole night, those are the eyes which used to believe that Ankhi's eyes are much better than him which used to make him happy and proud, the eyes will feel sorry for Akash but simultaneously the eyes will feel a satisfaction also because they are fulfilling the wish of Akash ,they are serving for Ankhi . Those are the eyes with which today Ankhi has seen Akash. The eyes today has got their right place but the heart does not, these are the eyes which used to give pleasure, peace and happiness to the heart starring at Ankhi, the eyes has left the heart today, the heart will be now more lonely than earlier, the heart will feel more pain than earlier,

Akash has not written anything about why he and Ankhi could not be life partners, in one of those diaries, he has written only one line ---"she has rejected me", but why Ankhi rejected Akash was not written there.

I can wish, I can wish for Akash, I wish...if suddenly it happens that the lips of Ankhi ask her eyes---"how you feel to be so close to me? I know how much you love me".

One day the nose of Ankhi will say her eyes---"I know, you believe that I am the best in the world".

One day the ears of Ankhi will say her eyes---"I know, you never choiced any ring for me ,because you think that if I wear ring then the ring will look better being attached with me"

One day the hair of Ankhi will say her eye---"I know when I come in front of you, you feel the happiest moment of life."

The eyes are so lucky, Akash never got a loving touch of Ankhi but his eyes will get. Akash has never got a hug from Ankhi but his eyes will get ...whenever Ankhi will blink, her eyes will get hug of her eyelash, and a huge hug during night, every night.

I don't know hearing all these; the eyes will feel how much happiness now, because now it's not connected to the heart of Akash. Now it's connected with Ankhis's heart, and probably one day Ankhi will love herself much more than now, because those are the eyes which showed Akash that how much beautiful mind Ankhi has, the sweet nature of Ankhi, I know, one day will come when the eyes will be mad being apart from Akash, then Ankhi will realize how much love Akash had for her, one day she will surely realize, I don't know when that day will come, I don't know till then Akash will survive with the so much pain or not. I know now the days are like hell to Akash, he has sacrificed his heaven for her whom Akash sees as an angel, probably this angel will feel one day that what a precious gift she has got from God ,One day will surely come because love can conquer everything.

The Unspoken

...True love needs no words

Jyotirmoy Sarkar

Chapter---1

Diya's Diary

After three days I will get married but the truth is I still love Akash and will love him for the rest of my life. From last two years I am always wishing that something miraculous happens and we become together. I knew there is less possibility of it but except wishing I had no other way left. I can't propose him because I can't make his life in trouble. I have myself broken many proposals of my marriage, my family members have become irritated for my such behavior, its natural, they are worried about my future, except my mom only Dipa knows about my love . Mom used to make me understand that it's not possible that Akash can be mine even she also told me that though Akash is genuinely a good human being but mom has objection because of his disease of which he came out two years ago. Time was passing, with every day passing my love for Akash was increasing but due to some emotional pressure I had to be agreed for my marriage.

From last two years I am living with his memories, every moments that I had spent with him are the sweetest moments of my life. After being detach with him I have never met him,

I can't do that but each and every day from last two years I have tried to feel those moments as I used to feel being with Akash. Sometime I have visited that park and especially that bench at exactly that time of the evening when we used to spent time with each other. Sometime sitting in that bench I used to buy   ice cream to cherish those moments when Akash used to laugh seeing my reaction for the coldness of the ice cream. There is not a single night in last two years when I have not talked with Akash seeing his picture. Sometime I have waited in that place where we used to meet, expecting that if by chance he comes to meet me, I knew very well that it's impossible but still I hoped and wished so. Sometime I have sung those songs which we used to sing together. Sometime singing the female voice I used to expect that suddenly I will hear his voice but it did not happen. I can't forget him, I can remember each and every moment and each and every words of Akash related to those moments. Even today I went to that park ,sat on that bench and closing my eyes I have wished that when I will open my eyes I will find Akash is sitting beside me and I will see his cute and nice smile again, but it did not happen. From last two years whenever I have got any message in my phone I have opened it expecting Akash has sent it but it has not happened. I know my words are sounding like mad but all these I am doing and expecting from last two years. I don't know what the end of my love is but I know that I will love Akash till my end. Yes it's true that I am compelled to marry some other guy but I can't live those dreams with some other one which I and Akash dreamt together. Situation has forced me to go far away from Akash but I am not selfish because my heart knows full well that his love for me was pure and unconditional, I know whenever he will remember me he will wish good for me.

With every morning I have raised expecting and wishing for his come back and in every night I have went to sleep with a broken heart, doing this from last two years my heart has made up and broken again and again but still it has not stopped beating for Akash.

Chapter---2

Dipa's Diary

After three days Diya will get married , it's not at all a good news neither for me nor for Diya, because its more than two years Akash Da has became well and it's also more than two years Diya loves him, but there is no way so that any relation can be made between them.

I came to know about Diya's love suddenly.....one year ago in the day of Akash Da's birthday, Aunty (Akash Da's Mom) and I went to temple to worship God in the name of Akash Da, there was a huge rush in the temple, I took the puja thali and managed to meet the priest, there was a girl who was also worshipping, the priest asked that girl---in whose name the puja will be given?

The girl replied---Akash Bose

Hearing the voice I became shocked…it was Diya.

Diya saw me when the priest asked me after asking her and I told the same name.

Diya had nothing to hide from me, coming out from temple I met her in the backward garden of the temple, we both were silent, we both were finding it tough how to start and what to say, then I asked---from when?

Diya replied---in those four months.

I said--- you know that neither we nor you can tell Akash Da about your love.

---yes I know.

---so what will happen now.

Diya replied---I will love him for the rest of my life, if my love is true then one day we will surely be together.

---you know it's almost impossible.

---yes I know.

Today the incident is coming into my memory when Diya's love story met an end, that day was one of the most happiest day in my life until I came to know about Diya's love for Akash Da, that day Akash Da became completely well but now I can realize that ---that is the day when Diya's love story met an end.

This love story started two years and four months ago……..in an evening Aunty called me over phone and requested to visit their home as soon as possible. Akash Da is not my own brother, we don't share any blood relation also, he is the friend of my brother Shubho Da ,their friendship started ten years ago and gradually developed into a very good relation between Akash Da and our family. Akash Da is a lecturer of literature.

I immediately visited Akash Da's home with my husband Ranjan and sister-in-law Rita, we noticed uncle and aunty is correct Akash Da has got a brain disorder; they were watching Akash Da from the morning and after being sure they called me.

From the morning Akash Da had confined himself in his room, sometime angrily murmuring and violently shouting and breaking the furniture's of his room. He was reluctant to talk with anyone, even if we were calling him he started to shout very loudly. We did not know what to do. Whole night we spent sitting outside Akash Da's room and expecting he will open the door but it did not happen, that was a sleepless night for all of us. I called my dada, he was in Mumbai for a meeting, and he reached in the next morning. Thank to God that Akash Da responded to dada, though he was unable to recognize dada but he was listening to him .Then for next forty five days we visited all the famous doctors of India, but no medicines had worked, it appeared that the medicines just vanishes after entering the stomach of Akash Da, during night Akash Da used to be more violent that's why high dose sleeping injection was must for his sleep. After forty five days we were planning to visit foreign doctors, we all gathered in Akash Da's home for discussion. That day a girl, approximately 28 years of age visited us. After exchanging greetings she told about herself.

---my name is Diya Bannerjee, I am a student of Prof. Baksi, he is the professor of psychology and the colleague of Mr. Bose. Mr. Bose used to visit Prof. Baksi because he has huge interest in psychology and he used to like to listen the discussions of Prof. Baksi and his students, Prof. Baksi helps his students in research. I have come to know about Mr. Bose's condition from Prof. Baksi.

Dada asked ---so how can we help you?

--- I am researching on brain disorder, I have come to know that you are preparing to visit foreign , I thought that you need time to make arrangements so I will request you to give me a chance in between these days ,the maximum negative result can be ---I will fail, nothing more than that, am I right?

 We took time to decide.

She was right, we need time to make the arrangements so we all decided to give her a chance. But the confusion was whether Akash Da will talk to her or not? Next day in the morning we informed our decision to Diya, in that evening Diya met us and took details about Akash Da.

 Dada told her ---generally Akash remains calm and quite during day time, sometime he spends all the day thinking deeply and talking to no one. He talks only with me and Dipa; there is no discipline--- when he takes food, when he takes bath. Sometime he talks with us for long time. His style of talking has become like a child.

Diya asked---what he talks about.

Dada said---he talks about famous authors, writers and poets, about their writings and their life histories.

Diya asked---does not he talk about psychology?

---yes he talks sometime but stops talking saying "what's the profit to discuss psychology with you, you possess no knowledge about it.

Diya took some more info and went away.

In the next morning Diya met me in Akash Da's home and told me...meet Mr. Bose and tell him ---one of my friends is researching on psychology and she needs your help.

I asked ---will it work?

She said---I hope so but it's also true that he will take a psychology test of mine.

The plan worked and Diya got chance to go closer to Akash Da.

Diya informed us that she will give us report after one month of treatment. For the first one month she used to visit Akash Da irregularly .sometime two days in a week sometime three days in a week. After one month she called all of us and said ---I think I can make Mr. Bose completely well; I need some more time .now decision is in your hand.

Diya was right, after one month of her coming we noticed much improvement in Akash Da's condition. So we agreed.

Diya took three more months for treatment, she did not inform anything, we just used to see improvement in Akash Da's condition and so we never disturbed her .in a morning Diya called me and told to keep free time in the afternoon because she can call us anytime.

She called us in the afternoon, reaching Akash Da's home we find him in senseless condition and admitted him in nursing home.

Later she explained us how she made the treatment----Diya always believed that mental shock is much more effective than electric shock because in mental shock there are emotions, feelings and desires are present and if these are broken ,then the effect is much effective than electric shock. The higher the emotions are the more effective the shock will be when those are broken

Diya started to create a sense in the mind of Akash Da that she loves him .when Akash Da started to feel Diya's deep love, he also fell in love with her. They never proposed each other. They had spent long tree months with love, when the belief of Akash Da about Diya's love became stronger then one day Diya called Akash Da in her home and shown him the fake pictures of her engagement that gave a huge blow in the faith, feelings and believe of Akash Da. He asked Diya the reason of betrayal, and then Diya made huge insult to Akash Da for his wrong thoughts. After that he came back home ,shouted ,murmured and then became senseless, we admitted him in nursing home and after long five hours he got sense with all body conditions normal, he became completely well, we all were present in the nursing home and except Diya we all met him. The memories of Akash Da during his disorder has been totally erased from his mind so we can't bring Diya in front of him because as per doctors advise if Akash Da sees Diya then he can get extreme stress in brain and any danger can happen, now I can realize that was the day when Diya's love met an end because in the process of doing fake love Diya started to love him truly.

Now I know about Diya's love but we all are helpless because neither can we tell Akash Da about Diya nor he can remember those Days.

Chapter---3

Dipa's Diary

Yesterday was the day of Diya's marriage, in the morning she called me over phone and told me---Dipa, I want a little favor from you.

I said---why are you saying so, you know we are indebted to you, you just say, if it's in my limit then I will surely do.

---for the last time I want to see Akash, you know I have to leave this city after my marriage and I don't know when will I get chance to see him, please do something for me.

---ok, let me make a plan and will inform you very soon.

Only one plan came into my mind...I called Akash Da and said ----can you please pick me while going university and drop me in the temple, my car has met a trouble.

---ok no problem sis, actually I will visit the temple also.

I informed Diya to come to the temple.

Akash Da was worshipping, the priest Asked ---in whose name the puja will be done?

Akash Da said---Diya Bannerjee.

hearing his answer I became so much astonished that I was almost being senseless, being normal I was about to leave the place to find Diya and inform her but Akash Da caught my hand and stopped me. Looking at me and moving his head he just instructed me to not to do that.

I had nothing to do except making prayer. Probably that time I have made the deepest prayer of my life. Water was coming out from my eyes recklessly. If at that time I were in a lonely place and no one around me then I would surely cry out shouting with all my energy.

The priest Asked Akash Da---who is she, any relative?

There was a pin drop silence for a while and then I heard a female voice saying---she is his would be wife and surely will be.

Then they faced each other, they both were crying and me also. Probably ten minutes has passed and then Diya said---you are a mad.

Akash Da replied---that's the reason I never expressed my feelings, can anyone love a mad?

Diya hugged him and said---yes, another mad.

#####

Half-Brother

- Vatsal Shah

As Akshay climbed the stair to his cabin on first floor of the office building in his factory, he gaped at the huge photo of Gandhi in his good-nature smile. It was placed on huge empty wall that formed the backdrop of the stair by Akshay's father Mr. Sudhanshu Jagat, who was an ardent fan of Gandhi, or rather a devoted worshipper. Some lines were written on the adjoining space, saying that the customer was the most important person on the premises... and so on.

It was Tuesday and Akshay knew that his father would have a very busy schedule to the extent that he would allow meetings to roll over the lunch table. Mr. Sudhanshu Jagat loved to be the head and chairperson and was rightly invited by various prestigious institutions to take charge of them. Amongst it was the Gujarat Institue of Industry, where he was the president. He even ran a charitable eye- hospital for the down-trodden, and was the trustee in a temple, and President in the Indo-French Council, and in the Lotus Club and in the Rotary, and if we try to enlist more the whole story would be filled with the list. Their factory produced industrial machinery for the plastic industry. It was a great set-up duely developed and nutured by Akshay's father, who had built it almost from scratch to the few hundred crore industry that it was now.

It was going to be a busy day. Akshay was rushing through his incomplete presentation. The convention of Plastic Industries Trade Association (PITA) was around the corner. It was this weekend in Banglore. He had to finnish the presentation for it of their company. The phone rang. It was his father, "There is a nice person, I would like you to meet. Please come to my cabin." Akshay many a times felt frustrated as out of the blue Mr. Jagat would call, when Akshay was busy with some work, and then the whole schedule would be disrupted as Mr. Sudhanshu had a habit of asking for reports and getting lost in minor details and nitti grittis and go wildly off-track, and waste a lot of time.

"I am preparing the presentation for PITA. Can't it wait till after one or two hours. We can meet when I am done." Akshay said politely but firmly.

"No it can't. Please come now." Mr. Sudhanshu said and the phone went dead.

Akshay thinking it was urgent rushed to his father's office. He was surprised to see a boy waiting there, along with his father. The boy looked hardly twenty one years of age. He was fair and his eyes were light grey. Surprisingly like Mr. Sudhanshu Jagat's.

"This is Rumit. He has done his MBA from Pune, and right now is about to give his final CA exams. He is brilliant. I have checked his records. He has been strongly recommended by our CA, Mr. Gagdekar. I suggest that you meet him, have a detailed talk to him about how he can be useful to our company. I would like him to personally assist me and work in close connection with Rakeshbhai, our financial manager."

Akshay was shocked. The financial manager's work was the most confidential. He had all the figures of the factory, and he never had any assistant. He would be reporting directly to the owners. If anyone joined him, he would know all the financial in and outs of the factory.

"We would need to discuss this, " Akshay looked his father in the eye, trying to explain the situation without speaking. But his father was too busy looking at some papers on his desk from the Chambers of Industry and other organizations which were always ready to take him on a rollercoaster ride.

"Ok, Rumit please come to my cabin after half an hour", Akshay said.

"Why not now?" Mr Sudhanshu asked. "Relieve him so he can go for his studies..."

"I have half an hours work left on the presentation." Akshay said firmly, as he knew when to put his foot down.

Rumit came to Akshay cabin after waiting for half and hour. He carried his Curriculam Vitae and some certificates from the Institution he had studied. Akshay was surpised that the boys father had long since been dead, and so was his mother. Late Mr. Bipinchandra. "I am sorry", Akshay said, "about your father."

"Actually my father left me and my mom, when I was 5 to 6 years of age. He left us our home and a lot of money, we could live by. I don't remember much of him, except that he loved me a lot, and the gifts he had given me on all my birthdays till I was 5 years of age. I don't recall his face much.

My mom had to put up this fake name in schools and other places. She told me, she would never give his name. Mom died last year," and he broke up. Akshay passed on the tissue to him.

"She gave me a letter to Mr. Gagdekar. It was a sealed envelope. I don't know it's content. But Mr. Gagdekar on reading it phoned Mr. Jagat and recommended me for a job."

"Since Mr. Gagdekar is our close associate, we would definitely honor his recommendation and keep you on trial basis for 3 months. And if everything goes well, we will make you permanent.

***

Akshay felt something was surely not in place somewhere. How could a newcomer get so much recommendation from everyone. He called up Kush, who was his personel manager. Kush was unmarried with long face, unshaven mostly from a day or two's stubble. He would love to have the haggard look and as if he had not groomed since two days. When he turned up clean shaven and in ironed up clothes, Akshay would feel he is seeing some animal. Though his haggard appearance Kush was very particular about everything in his manner. He had dexersity about having every nick and nack in order, all papers, all to-do-lists, and the factory in general. He would often waste a lot of expensive time in discussing such trivial details with Akshay and his father. Through his such manners he had become Mr. Sudhanshu Jagat's pet.

"I want you to keep a check on this new fellow, what is his name, Rumit. I want you to do more than that. Check out his bio-data. Get his hand-writting analysed. As we sometimes do with our new-comers. Get his brain-mapping done from his finger-prints. Now don't ask me how you will manage that. Tell him we do it with employees to know their aptitude. Find out all you can about him from his past records. Whatever information you can get from his college, ex-school, his face-book page, etc. I think I don't have to teach you anything. You are an expert and you know that." Akshay said firmly but politely and added, "And make sure Mr. Sudhanshu Jagat knows nothing about this." Kush was wondering what was going on. Why this detective novel style investigation. But he knew very well that he has to please Akshay as well as he was his father's pet. Mr. Jagat would retire in a few years and then Akshay would be the boss. And with his expertise in no particular field except being an obedient 'yes-man', he had no portfolio to boast about or get an equally paying job.

As Akshay got busy with PITA convention, he forgot all about Rumit for a few days. Then Akshay was out of town and when he returned, he inquired how Rumit had been doing.

"He is smart, and eager to learn," told Mr. Rakesh the financial manager. "He is the only person who directly reports to Mr. Jagat, as per Mr. Jagat's instructions." Akshay was furious. No one was allowed to see their personal accounts and hardly anyone except the senior managers reported directly to Mr. Jagat. He was wondering why all this kindness and generousity was being bestowed on Rumit.

Akshay called Kush to his cabin.

"The boy was born in Pune. He studied at St. Francis school in Pune. A catholic school. He got good grades. He was a smart chap since Kindergarten..., " Kush started.

"Cut the crap," Akshay snapped, "I haven't got all day."

"He graduated and did Masters in Business Administration from Pune University. He is from a lower middle class family. His mother Kumudini was a beautiful lady. She took tutions of high school students. Rumit lived off from some income of his mother and through interests of FD's in his and his mother's name in a bank in Pune. His shirt size is 42. His shoe size is no.7. He doesn't seem to have a girlfriend, is single, and probably a virgin..."

"You f**kwit. This is not the information I wanted. You got me all crap. Who is the boy's father?" Akshay got to the point.

"Mr. Bipinchandra, that is what is mentioned in his birth-certificate and his school leaving certificate and other documents. But no one knows who this Mr. Bipinchandra is. I have been inquiring with our dealers in Pune, about Rumit's background. They are suspicious why we want all this information. No one knows about any Mr. Bipinchandra. He is a mystery. Probably as Rumit says, he died, or left him and his mother when Rumit was too young or Rumit is a b**tard, and his mother was not married in the first place." Kush reported.

"You have now come to the point. I want you to go to Pune under any pretence and get me information about Rumit's family, in particularly his father. You can go to the address. Take help of our dealers there. But you will get two to three days maximum. I can't let you be away from the factory without Mr. Jagat being suspicious about what is going on.

**

That day it rained. It was rain in May, in Ahmedabad, where it would otherwise be scorchingly hot summer going on. But it was the North-westerlies reported the media. Akshay came home tired. His sprawling mansion was right in the middle of the Central Business District. But well buffered with trees and flowering shrubs. The peacocks came there and danced. Akshay's mother Sejal was an environmentalist, plant biologist. She did free-lance research work for various organizations. They were developing cross-breed and hybrid plants.

"It is a pity it is so stormy today," Sejal told Akshay as he entered the house. She was tending a bonsai sort of plant. We are trying to breed a rare colour of bouganville, deep orange. And when it seems this plant will flower, it rained. Bouganvilles need dry weather to flower..." She kept chatting.

"So what are news of our factory," she asked Akshay, and what is our Mr. Details, I mean Kush up to?

"Oh! him. He has gone to Pune on some business. Meetings with our dealers. Finding new clients in that area," Akshay replied.

"But we don't need to do that. You probably would not be knowing, because you were five years at that time. Your Daddy had a branch factory at Pune. He went there every month. Stayed for three to four days and sometimes a week there. People know him very well there. All dealers and customers. You don't need to start from scratch at Pune," Sejal was saying. Akshay was surprised but managed well to hide his wonder.

"I think the demand was not so much in those days, and we were able to produce machinery from here itself, so your Dad wound up the factory at Pune. But he did fondly remember it many a times. He told me how the weather in Pune was so pleasant and the greenery there, and you could go to the hills nearby and see the water-falls and rivulets and be with nature..." Sejal was chatting away, her good self as usual, "but I think your Dad never thought of reviving the factory there."

***

Kush had returned from his Pune trip. He sat in Akshay's cabin, " I have got news that will rock you off the chair. We had a branch factory in Pune 27 years back. Rumit's mother Kumudini worked in the Admin department as the chief administrator. She was never married. I could not trace her marriage record in the Memorandum of Marriages of Pune. She delivered Rumit at the Lakeview Hospital there. I inquired with some of the doctors there. It was such an old matter, they hardly recalled anything, but that Rumit's mother had wanted an abortion, but it was way past the safe date. No father of Rumit visited them. Yes, Mr. Jagat paid for her hospital as she was our employee and in need of money. Now if you want to know more about Rumit's background, or his mother, I think the best person you can ask is Mr. Jagat."

Akshay was furious. "Was he putting two and two together? Who was this boy Rumit? Was he his half-brother?" Akshay lost himself in thoughts. He realized quiet late that Kush had already left his cabin. He then heard Mr. Jagat yelling, and rushed outside in the corridor. Mr. Jagat's cabin was the only one which was a closed cabin with no glass. So Akshay put his ear to the door, to eavesdrop about what was going on.

"So Kush you went to Pune," he was yelling, "without informing me. We have so much of work pending. And I got phone-calls from some of my old acquaintances there. You were inquiring about our old factory there and about the staff there, and where I was living and what I was doing there... Is that what you are paid for, to spy on me? You are having fun at the company's expense. I warn you clearly, that next time you do that, you will find yourself sitting at home, doing your detective work."

Kush came out dejected and was surprised to find Akshay so near the door. Kush looked like a kid in kindergarten who had got a good spanking. "I am out of it," he told Akshay, "you please ask someone else to do all this dirty job." Kush was almost at the verge of tears and Akshay found himself a second time in one week offering a tissue to someone across the table.

**

"One last favour for me," Akshay told Kush. "I want a DNA strain test done of Rumit and of Mr. Jagat. I want both the reports and names of expert genetic doctors who can infer from the reports."

"Are you trying to insinuate that Mr. Jagat is Rumit's fa...." Kush stopped short of completing the sentence.

"Mr. Kush, I guess you should keep to doing what you are told." Akshay snapped. Kush left. Rumit was asked to a regular body profile check-up by Mr. Kush. He told him that the company cared for their employees and more than a formality it was the company's generosity. Kush had no guts to ask Mr. Jagat. He had made this clear to Akshay and Akshay had told him that he would take care of that part.

***

It was warm and sunny. The nor-westerly's had passed. Sejal was tending the bougainvillea, which had started flowering deep orange. Sudhanshu was at the breakfast table, reading the paper and making a call at one time and looking into the mobile appointment reminders. Akshay never liked all this on the breakfast table, but couldn't say anything. Sudhanshu got up and in a rush to climb the stairs to his room, slipped and fell near the stairs.

"Pappa, how many times I have told you to get a complete body profile done. You might be having low sugar. Your diabetes was not in control last time. Your SGPT, lipid profile...", Akshay started.

"Oh no! It is the water from the Bougainville bonsai, overflowed near the steps. I slipped on it." Mr. Jagat was saying. But Akshay told him that he would have none of his excuses. He would be calling the lab, where they get reports done of everyone in the factory to collect blood after lunch in the afternoon.

***

"How much is my diabetes?", Mr. Sudhanshu Jagat was roaring at the attendant of the lab on phone, who had not found his reports. Mr. Jagat felt he was obliging the lab enough by giving it so much work, that he should have quick service from them, at least for his own reports.

"Sir! I found it. Your report is here and ready with us! Your body profile. Your diabetes is normal, so is the SGPT and lipid profile in control. We have not got your DNA report till now, from the genetic lab."

"What DNA report?" Jagat grew suspicious.

"We had a request for two DNA reports. Your's and some employees. Let me see the name... Rumit," the attendant stuttered.

"F**k you all, what exactly is going on? Who asked for the DNA report? Give it to Roopal, the head pathologist there. It is time I give her a piece of my mind."

***

Akshay's mobile rang. He had come to Jabalpur to meet some old customers. He saw it was his father on the line. His father was shouting and it could be heard by the customers. So Akshay excused himself and went out of the conference room in which they were having a meeting.

"What exactly is going on?" Mr. Jagat roared. "A detective story. A spy thriller. I am being spied on. First you send Kush to Pune to inquire about our old factory and where I was staying and all, and now you have under the pretext of diabetes, got a DNA scan of my blood sample!"

"Stop shouting," Akshay said calmly, "it is you who I should be asking a few questions..." He hung up.

***

The next day Akshay was back home. On the breakfast table. Mr. Jagat was his jolly good self. Reading the paper, making some phone-calls, arranging his schedule. Akshay avoided speaking anything. Neither did he feel his father wanted to talk about anything. "Can you pass me the butter?" was all Mr. Jagat told Akshay on the breakfast table.

After he reached office and by noon, was through with his routine, Akshay thought of calling the pathological lab. The attendant told him that they had a small fire at the lab and all the samples taken in the last two days were damaged and all reports soiled up. Akshay quickly called up Kush to inquire about Rumit.

"Rumit left yesterday. You were at Jabalpur and it was not such an important matter to disturb you there," said Kush, who was otherwise reporting all trivial details. "He told us that he was going to join a pharmaceutical company in Gantok, Sikkim. He left rather abruptly and has not asked for his month's salary."

It would me many days later that Akshay would find out that the pharmaceutical company Kush had mentioned never existed in Sikkim. No one would know what happened with Rumit. And many years later Akshay would find that in this period of hodge-podge, a deal had been signed by Mr. Jagat. He had sold off some important property, worth enough money to last a person his lifetime, and where the money was transferred no one knew.

#####

MASTANI

-A.K.Sinha

(PROLOGUE--The Peshwas had a special love for Paithani textiles. "Paithani" is derived from the small town Paithan located in Central India, Maharashtra state, about 400 km north east of Bombay. During the 17th century, the Mughal emperor Aurangzeb patronized the Paithani Silk weavers and introduced new motif that was called Aurangzebi.

A 'Peshwa' is the equivalent of a modern Prime Minister. They were leaders in military expeditions ,great strategist and expanded Maratha Empire. The founder of the Maratha Empire Chatrapati Sibaji, created the 'Peshwa' designation in order to more effectively delegate administrative duties.

Mastani was the second wife of Peshwa Baji Rao I (1700–1740), a Maratha general and prime minister to the fourth MarathaChhatrapati. Mastani was a courageous lady worked for education of girl Childs and helped his husband in running their states. The following is a Historical fictional story involving the above places and characters)

*****

Today Abha took leave from the field earlier for getting ready to negotiate with the cotton traders. She sat by the banks of the great river Godavari thinking the strategy they

75

should adopt to counter the low price offered by the Royal Munshi. She wanted to dress and look properly when dealing with those rich miser traders who look down upon the girls. Minutely she was removing the cotton fragments from the body, wash hair with soap and wear fresh clothes. So unabashedly she stripped down in the lonely bank, washed her clothes and was half way through her bathing when the boat came within the sight.

'I am sick of this!' she grunted loudly as she sighted the boat.

The familiar boat can be identified by its white sail. They came early today. 'I hate their lustful eyes, they seem too hungry; what should I do now? How do I get my clothes?'

She tried to climb the banks hurriedly to get her clothes lying in a bundle. But the boat came nearer with the favourable wind. She made a dash for the nearest tree to hide. There were catcalls and whistles from the boat. She could spot the old trader Patil grazing her with his greedy eyes. Finally, she could hide behind a tree and cover her modesty.

Shockingly up there, a gentleman was silently watching the proceedings from a horseback. Abha turned back saw him and felt helpless. She placed her hands as a cover. The gentleman looked tall with cropped hair, fair and handsome. He came down closer to her. 'I warn you not to come closer.' Abha grasped the knife in her bundled cloth. Still he didn't stop. Abha removed her hand and took out the knife. The rider paid no heeds. He came closer, and took out his long white scarf. His bare well-built body mesmerized Abha. He came one step closer; wrapped the scarf around her, turned back and rode away. Abha was in a state of be wilderness and stood there motionless. The scarf still has the fragrance of the owner.

By afternoon, all the women workers with cotton bales gathered there. After a month's toiling, they carefully plucked the cotton from the field and bundled them expecting a good return. Many of them has still cottons covering their faces, body and stuck in hair. But a surprise was waiting for the traders. Appeared a gleaming Abha in a good paithan saree wrapped like traditional Dhoti much like the male folk, with a matching blouse on top. The ladies present there appreciated her style of wearing the sari as they would be much comfortable wearing like that when they work in the fields. All eyes were trained on her at once. The Munshi called her in a false tone of admiring and invited her to sit beside her. She unhesitatingly accepted the offer and sat face to face with the Munshi. 'So Patil sab what is the price you are offering today?'

Lowering his voice, he told 'For you I have two Roman gold coins, one coin per 100 bales but one extra for you.'

'Is it? Will you please stand up and announce?' The Munshi obliged. She slapped him in full view of public. Munseef fell down, taken by surprise. 'How dare you hit me trifle unchaste woman? I am a respectable person and can strip you at this market and buy you thousand times. I have a few slaves like you.' The Munshi shouted.

'I see, you consider yourself a respectable person who strips women in Marketplace, but don't threaten me that. Try at your peril; I will teach you a good lesson and make you run without clothes. From now onwards pay one gold coin for fifty bales or don't come here.' Turning to the assembled cotton pluckers, she said. 'Don't sell if you don't get fair price.'

It was a long-standing demand of the cotton pluckers of Sauviragram. They knew that the cotton fetches four times of what they get paid.

The Munsi said, 'Then eat those cotton, we will not buy at that price; let our Peshwa Damaji Rao Gaikwad Come. I will tell him how wicked and greedy you all have become.'

The waiting for the Peshwa was short lived. He arrived riding his horse and strode to the bidding table with a hand on his sword. The Munshi stood up and offered his chair and whispered in his ear all the demands made to him. There was all round silence. The Peshwa said something which appeared to change the face line of Munshi. He hesitatingly announced 'Ok for this time only you will get the enhanced price.'

Abha loudly said, 'Then don't come here next time,' having said so, she glanced to the Peshwa. He is the same gentleman who gave his scarf to cover her modesty. The Peshwa also noticed her. He was pleasantly surprised. He has never seen such a courageous woman who can boldly face a Man with a bare body and ask men folk for the legitimate rights. 'Ok, from now onwards you will get the fair price. Can I know your leaders name?' He had her eyes fixed on Abha. She came forward and stood with her hands on the waistband. 'I am Abha.., what's yours?' 'I am a Peshwa, Damji Rao.' 'So glad to meet you, bank on me; a Peshwa never goes back on his word.'

Who is this fearless lady? Born to a cotton merchant family, Abha has one younger brother shoal, who goes to school. But Abha was not sent to school by her family because she is a girl child. She pleaded with her parents for schooling without success because her parents were afraid of the social stigma. Instead, she was sent for working in the field from the age of ten to help her mother in plucking cotton. Now her mother doesn't go to the field, so Abha had to go to field and pluck cotton. His father bundles them at home.

In the night Abha listens attentively to Upanishad, read in Sanskrit and well explained by her grandpa, who is a big scholar in Sanskrit. He teaches Abha about the importance of woman in a family and the need for her education. He also tells that women were revered in ancient India unlike now, which is the result from various invaders barbaric and ill-treatment of ladies. This has been adopted by many men in our times. He had also trained Abha how a thread can be made from cotton by the wheel and spindle. Abha took the cue from him and managed to get the thread making wheels from Paithan and started making threads at home. This gradually spread to other pluckers and soon a sizeable number of them spun threads. Abha took the initiative of contacting weaving community at Paithan and sold cotton thread to them directly, thus earning more for the cotton produced by the villagers of Sauviragram.

Next month when the trading boat anchored, a big surprise was waiting for the Munshi. Few raw cotton sellers were there that too they are not agreeable to sell at the old rate. Abha was there leading them. She reminded Munshi about the commitment of the Peshwa.

The Peshwa arrived late through a different route and didn't go the trading ground. He visited the fields and found girls spinning wheels to produce threads. Moving in disguise, he found Abha is the moving force behind them. He remembered she is the same lady whom he first meets in a rather peculiar situation. Her statue-like figure was engraved in his mind. She seemed straight from the Greek pillars which adorn the palaces of emperors. He decided to marry her. He went straight to her house, meets her parents, and asked for their permissions and blessings.

It was a moment of joy for the family and Abha's father couldn't believe that his daughter is going to marry a Peshwa. He did his best to put up a good show to marry off their daughter to a Peshwa dynasty. Many of the villagers were invited, and they were pleased to see their loving daughter is married to a Royal family.

Abha did not want only to decorate his husband's house as a beautiful wife, so she asked Damji's concurrence to allow her to take an active part in outside work. First she toured various villages and ensured cotton is bought at fair prices. She knew this plucking is done mainly by the women folk, so she arranged to teach them how to make threads from cotton and do a value addition. Abha also ensured people like the ex-munshi did not get a chance to exploit women in particular. She declared that girls under the age of 18 will not pluck cotton and they should go to school.

She did not get a chance to study in school as per the prevailing customs, keeping this in mind she asked her husband for grant of money to set up a few Sanskrit schools for girls. This school was dedicated in the name of her grandpa Gajendra Patil who gave her insights into Upanishads and the rights of women.

Since her husband was a Peshwa, for many days he would have stayed at the battlefields, during this time she would look after the day- to- day affairs of the estate and she often visited many schools and persuaded parents to send their daughters to school for education.

But life changed suddenly. Her husband once returned from the tour with a woman as his second wife. The woman was Narayan bai and was having a daughter.

'Why the hell you bought that woman?' 'I have not bought; I have conquered her with the kingdom.' 'So you murdered her husband. Why did you do that?'

'That's the way Peshwa's rule, why you are so annoyed?'

'You will not do this again or I will kill the woman accompanying you.'

The Woman Narayan Bai has none virtues except her sex appeal and appeared to charm Damaji Rao by offering her wild sex, wine and sometimes other women. In the mean time, Abha gave birth a son but this alarmed Narayan bai very much.

Being a woman, Abha did not want to hurt her instead she pleaded with Narayan bai not to indulge in drinking with her husband in the company of other women, but she appeared not to pay any heed.

One day in the evening when she heard loud music from the mazlis, she decided to intervene. Dance by a young girl with scanty clothes was in full swing in the hall. She got very much disturbed when she found that Narayan Bai accompanied by her Ten-year-old daughter was enjoying the show.

'Stop all this and please go to your respective places,' she told the gathering in a farm voice. Narayan bai shouted,'Who the hell are you? Do you think yourself Mastani?' Narayan bai came forward in a drunken state. Abha slapped her twice. She fell flat on the ground. 'Please don't degrade your-self,' exclaimed Abha and turned to her husband.

'Come Damaji don't spoil your name, I will not let you spoil yourself and your estate like this, you have enormous responsibility on your shoulder.'

Damaji was not in a state to respond but followed her silently. From that day, she guarded Damaji so that he shouldn't get back to old habit of drinking. Narayan Bai from that day thought of taking revenge but couldn't do anything except anger flaming her mind. Years rolled by, but Narayan Bai did not change. She hatched up a plan to eliminate her son by poisoning his milk.

Glasses of milk in breakfast table was a must item, a fovourite drink for Abha's son. Narayan bai one day poisoned it with arsenic. Somehow the glasses got exchanged. Damji in a hurry consumed the milk from the glass which was poisoned. He collapsed on the table and died. Sentries came running and closed all the exits. But nobody could be held responsible although Abha had doubted the involvement of Narayan Bai.

In the evening, pyres were lighted and Abha asked his son to complete the last rights. She was keeping a tab on Narayan bai and got her room thoroughly searched. A bottle of arsenic was found there, and it was tested on a stray dog that instantly collapsed dead.

Next day she called a meeting of the satraps and asked Narayan Bai to be present there with her daughter. The meeting began with a condolence for the departed Peshwa. Abha spoke with a choked voice, 'It is very unfortunate that a Peshwa had to die in a breakfast table. The murderer is amongst us.' She paused and looked at Narayan Bai, 'I want no further bloodshed and enimity. From now onwards the day-to-day works of our kingdom will be carried out jointly by my son Baji Rao and daughter Arzoo,' she declared, there was a murmur amongst the gathering as Abha's son was the natural heir to the Peshwa.

Abha walked to the throne with the children on her both sides.

#####

When Feeling Turn Around!!

-Mitushree

What else she needs when she has a cup of coffee in her hand and one old diary. Suddenly it starts raining which takes her to the flashback, a year ago.

And the flashback begins from the day; I met him.

That day I was lost somewhere. That feeling is special when you realize that you fell in love with your bestfriend. I was the happiest person ever. In my deep thoughts, I was thinking about him. I got lost in the world of him. That day I met him for the first time. We talked and became friends. With the passing of time, good friends to close friends and then at last best friends forvever. We used to talk for hours. He knew everything from my past to my future dreams. My smallest lie to my biggest secrets. Yes, he knew everything. We used to fight on silly reasons. We used to cry for each other. I never got to know when this friendship turned into love. The guy I just met three months ago was in love with me. One day while we were talking; he said, "Muje tum se kuch khena hai".

"Ha bolo na", I said.

"Just promise me that nothing will change between us. ",Armaan said.

"Hmm sochna padega". I tried to pull his leg.

"I am serious Anamika." Armaan said.

"Oops okay baba sorry bolo ab kya bolna hai? sirf 5 min hai tumhare pass." I said laughingly.

"I love you. I really do love you", He said nervously.

" I know tu shocked hogi but bhot dino se bolne ka try kar raha hun but nai mauka mila. And I won't force you up for anything. Hum friends thay hai aur hamesa rahenge. Take your time and think. "He said.

"Thank you Armaan. ",I said.

I thought a lot about this and I realized that somewhere even I was in love with him too. Before I met him, I was fine but he made me realize that even I can smile. Yes, i fell in love with my best friend. It is truly said that if you really love someone you don't need to be lovers. He loves me and so do I. And we both fell in love with our friendship. He became that important part of my life's puzzle that can't be fixed by anyone else now. Just a thought of losing him and I was in pain.

Months passed. Everything was going on the track. From good morning to good night texts were going along with our love. Love was in the air. Sometimes I used to think about our future. It was 10 pm, I was on the bed waiting for his message. That day I was feeling a little low. Infinite thoughts were running in my mind. One by one every thought started attacking on my mind. Don't know why but yes I was little worried thinking about our future. Suddenly my cell beeped with his message.

" Hey ,ssup my gal?" He asked.

" Hmm...nothing much." I replied.

"Mood kyu off hai?" He questioned.

"Baby..." I said.

"Ya ?" He replied.

"Hamare parents maan toh jayenge na?" I asked worriedly.

"So yeh baat hai?" He asked.

"Ya", I replied.

" I promise I will do anything for us. Hamare parents ko hum milke manyenge. Sab aacha hoga." He said.

"I love you Armaan." Tears rolled down from my cheeks.

"I love you more." He said and abh rona band kar .

"Tuje kese pata ki mei roh rahi hun ?" I asked.

"Bas pata chala gaya connection you know and just listen to me." He said.

"Haan." I replied back.

" Kuch nahi bas yuhi. " He texted back.

Life was going good. Truly said three golden years of one's life are college days. Those going for movies spending time at cafe and group studies. Everything was just perfect.

* Few months later.*

I fell asleep while waiting for his message. When I woke up at midnight for water I texted him.

" Sorry ankh kab lagi pata nai chala." I mesaaged.

"That's okay." He said.

" Armaan is there something troubling you please let me know. You seems to quite annoyed and worried everytime." I messaged.

"Aisa kuch nai hai." He replied back.

"Please I just can't see you this way baby." I said.

"Anamika, I think its over now. We should maintain distance. There is no future of us. I know thodi problem hogi starting mei but fir sab thik ho jayega." He said

"What do you mean Armaan? Are you kidding me. And you promised me our future. I want to meet you tomorrow morning." I said.

"I can't. I can't see you crying in front of me." He said.

"Tum akele sab nai decide kr sakte ho." I said angrily.

"Mene jo bhi decide kia hai soch samajh k kiya hai." He said.

"It's too late we should sleep now." His message came.

:Hmmm." I replied.

"Good night. "He said.

I was completely blank. Tears were not ready to stop from my eyes. In just few moments I lost my best friend, my soulmate, my smile, my laugh and even myself. The worst nightmare I had ever. He left. I wished feelings would just die when a person leave you alone.

 Yes, heartbreaks changes people.

* 5 months later... *

Today I saw him after months. There was a girl beside him. His Fiance. Yes, it still hurts to see him with other girls. My heart beats fastened. We stood there, looking at each other but said nothing. It was like we meant nothing to each other. One girl and thousand feelings ran inside me.

Have you ever really wanted to ask a question, but you didn't because you knew in your heart that you won't be able to handle the answer? I wanted to ask him that if everything between us was real and true then how can he be just fine. But then then my heart screamed may be he was not ready for the kind of love that stays forvever. He used to say "Forever" love you, but look at us now we are strangers.

I still miss those days...

Those hours of chatting,Fighting over little things,Late night talks,Sharing secrets,Weird dreams,Being possessive,Attitudes,Waiting for one's texts,Watching one's pics and texting over and over, Smiling for no reason,Trusting him blindly,His hugs and kisses and his innocent wishes.

And now I am just having.

Blank inbox,No more I love you,Hours of lonliness,Unshared emotions,Late night cries,Heartbreaking secrets,Shattered dreams,Deleted memories,Fake smile,Broken trust and Devious heartaches...

And just like that everything we had, has died. I don't think it matters whether it is five days, five months or five years since your heart breaks you will feel miserable. I don't think it will really ever leaves you. Neither does it matter whether its relationship or friendship when it ends your heart does break.

Someday I will stop writing about you. But not today, because all my thoughts are still about you.

And today again tears rolled down. Diary got wet with his memories. There is nothing about writing you just have to sit near the typewriter and bleed and the emotions will flow.

#####

Rapunzel

-RiyaJain

This is the story of a girl whose name is Rapunzel Jackson born on 7th November 1997 (the same birthday as me.....). Her parents are Jimmy and Zoya Jackson. Jimmy Jackson is a renowned pop singer and an actor. He was crowned prince of pop in his school becoming the first pop singer and the monarch in his school. His school was made by his great-grandfather George Jackson in India. Jimmy Jackson was born on 1st of August 1970. This school is a boarding school. International students come and study in this school. In this school, it was made a rule that the heir of the owner George Jackson comes to school and is to be crowned the pop singer and the monarch of school. Now this is applied on every single person who is related or is the heir of George. George was made the first pop singer and the monarch of the school as he was the owner. He was already famous in the world because of being in the career since the age of 12 so he was crowned the king of pop but his successors would be first crowned pop princess or prince of pop the king/queen of pop. He died at the age of 100 when his great-grandson Jimmy Jackson our main character's father was in the school.

You might think what happened to Jimmy's grandfather and father. They both were not interested to study in that school and so studied in the local school in Gary Indiana but Jimmy was interested in this school. He wasn't told that his family owned the school and he was the heir as JImmy was interested in pop singing and was famous just because of his great-grandfather George Jackson's hard work. To know who was the heir of George Jackson, all the children good in singing and dancing- including Jimmy - were selected for 3 tasks to perform. 1st task:- Singing, 2nd task :- Dancing, and the 3rd task :- pop singing. Who would pass all 3 task would be the new pop singer and and the monarch. Jimmy and a friend of his, both passed all 3 tests so a final test would be conducted. This test stated that if 2 or more children passed all 3 tasks then the pop princess/pop prince crown would be placed on each of them till the crown grows when placed on the heir's head. And when the crown was placed on Jimmy's head, in few seconds. Now that he became the prince of pop, Jimmy understood that this was his family school and he was the heir of his great grandfather.

Years passed Jimmy became famous as a pop singer and an actor, he married Zoya Khan. In 1997 they were blessed with a boy named Jimmy Jackson Jr. on 18th April. Then they were blessed with a daughter Rapunzel Jackson on 7th November 1999. 3 years passed after that and in 2002, they got a letter:

"your daughter's destiny lies in India, send her to the school where you were crowned as king of pop"

but Jimmy told his wife Zoya to take it lightly because it might be a prank played by someone. But a year later, on Rapunzel's 4th birthday they got the same letter but with a warning:

"Don't waste your time, and this is not a prank your daughter's destiny really lies in India send her there".

They did Rapunzel to their school with Jimmy Jr. to take care of her. Years had passed, Zoya and Jimmy had come to India so that they could take care of both of their children. And it was the year, 2016. This year, the school crowns the heir after the 3 tasks even though they knew who was the heir. They had selected both Jimmy Jr. and Rapunzel but Jimmy Jr. stepped back for his little sister to be the heir because he knew that the school was owned by his family. Soon enough the tasks had started. Rapunzel was qualifying for the next tasks way too fast that means she was always the 1st one to be qualified in all 3 tasks. But She was not alone, she had another friend named Michelle Taylor. Both cable for being the next monarch but only one can be crowned as the next monarch. So the crowns was placed on both the girls' head. They all waited for one of the crowns to grow. A sudden flash came, hurting every one's eye expect... Rapunzel's...

Rapunzel's clothes changed from school uniform to a beautiful ball gown. It was soon clear to everyone that Rapunzel is not only the new monarch/pop princess but also a good actress.

A month later, there is an annual day of the school and Rapunzel and her elder brother, JImmy Jr., get the lead roles in the whole school play "Romeo and Juliet" (by the whole school I mean the grades from Grade 6 above as this is a love story grade 5 and below won't understand). The play was recorded by one of the parents of one of Jimmy Jr.'s friends.

All the parents in the school know that the school has a King and his Daughter the Princess of the music and the dance world and so are called Monarch of the popworld. They also know that Rapunzel is the pop princess of the school. The name of the school is Hogwarts International School and is truly an IB and IGCSE school. It runs both boards together and keeps the same rules for both the board students (the students studying in IB and IGCSE boards). Rapunzel was studying in IGCSE and so was her brother. The parent who was recording the play uploaded the 2 hour-long video on khaantube (this is an imaginary name don't mistake it with youtube) with the title "play of 'Romeo And Juliet' by the children of Hogwarts International School. The lead actors are Jimmy Jackson Jr. and Rapunzel Jackson children of the famous pop singer the king of pop Jimmy Jackson." This video was seen by all the fans of Jimmy Jackson including fans in India. Soon this video caught the eye of a famous Bollywood actor named Nyati Agarwal who was a living legend of the Indian Cinema. She now wanted to meet Rapunzel Jackson because Nyati found Rapunzel's acting amazing and extraordinary. She found the Rapunzel was totally into her character as if she was really Juliet. She went to Ahmedabad and found out Hogwarts International school.

That time it was Nyati's luck that it was a working day of the school and Rapunzel was there. To her surprise, Rapunzel was her only fan in the school and was inspired by Nyati herself for acting. Nyati told Rapunzel that Nyati was going to take Rapunzel to Bollywood shooting studio and sign Rapunzel for her first movie. And Rapunzel was very excited..

A few months later, Rapunzel's first movie "A special child - every child is special" was released. She was already famous for her pop singing. Now she was famous for acting too. Soon she got many offers of the movies but declined them all because of her studies, she also wanted to become a cook but because of being famous of acting and pop singing she did acting and pop singing courses in the universities.

Soon Rapunzel becomes a famous actor and pop singer. She is rising up like a spark. This was the year 2025, and she has decided to do a concert on the day of her birthday which is fortunately a Friday.She practices hard every day with the background singers and dancers and on her request her parents, her brother Jimmy Jr. and her godparents who are one of the famous actors in Hollywood to come for the concert. They did get backstage passes for free and were requested to come backstage to meet Rapunzel after the concert is over. The backstage passes were made on the request of Rapunzel. And these backstage passes were only limited in supply and would be or are given out by Rapunzel herself. She also had given a backstage pass to a winner in a contest on an interview show. That winner also got a VIP entry pass for the concert. All the VIP guests of the concerts had gotten the VIP entry pass and a backstage pass.

One day, during the rehearsals, as far as I remember, Rapunzel was rehearsing for the entry which was the opening act for the concert, Rapunzel had broken her hand. She had slipped down from the stage which helps her to go over the audience but it had no support for her to be safe. So she told her that she could do it without any safety. But the result of that confidence came out by making Rapunzel have facture in her hand. She was rushed to the hospital near the auditorium.While she was being checked and x-rayed, Rapunzel's facture got healed on it's own. The doctor treating Rapunzel- is the family doctor of the Jackson Family- said that It was a miracle because when someone had a fracture it took days, weeks or even months to be healed. Jimmy took Rapunzel back to the auditorium to makes sure that his daughter's rehearsals don't stop.

On the way Jimmy told Rapunzel that she possessed a special powers since her childhood even before being the pop princess of the school. That powers were passed down after the first pop singer of the school was crowned that is George Jackson. That crown kept on giving powers to him till Jimmy's grandfather wasn't born. After JImmy's grandfather was born, the powers were passed to him and were passed on to every child of the family. The people - who were crowned- were given more powers and were passed down to their children that means the powers that Jimmy had when he was crowned were passed down to Jimmy Jr., Rapunzel's elder brother, and Rapunzel is now that Rapunzel is crowned, she is getting more powers.
The school of theirs that is Hogwarts school was in a full tension because they don't have any heir to success Rapunzel. Rapunzel starts her rehearsals again. Months pass by, and each day Rapunzel did rehearsals. Finally, Rapunzel's birthday

had come which is also the day of the concert. Things were going well till Rapunzel was again fractured but she didn't mind. She continued with the concert. That was perfect timing of Rapunzel getting fractured again because that time her latest song fractured heart was going on. The concert ended with the song which Jimmy had sung. Singing this song, Rapunzel was giving tribute to her father who was her idol also.

After the concert, Jimmy ran to the backstage while Rapunzel's godparents, Zoya and Jimmy Jr. tried to stop but no one could. Jimmy was with happy tears. Rapunzel knew that her father would with happy tears and would be coming to hug her for thanking her to sing his song in front of her fans. Jimmy did go and hugged her with happy tears. That was the main motive of Rapunzel to make her father happy. That did happen but also it made the whole family happy. I think she might a reincarnation of George Jackson

.

So a year later, Rapunzel was accepted in a group named "loads remixed" which was Rapunzel's favourite group since she had heard their songs for the first time. She was happy that she was now a part of that group but she did many solo albums also when she and her other teammates weren't recording. So Rapunzel recorded her solo songs between the group's recording sessions. She didn't get time to get rest or to sleep.

After a few of the group albums, all the singers went on break saying that they all need a break after the albums they made. They needed this break to refresh their minds for new ideas for the songs. During the break, Rapunzel had fun, she stayed at home the whole day and fortunately, it was the month of December, and they had taken a break on 19th of December. Let me remind you this happened in the year 2026, a year after her concert on 7th November 2025. 5 days after, it was Christmas eve and Rapunzel had a greatest desire to celebrate Christmas with her family and she also invited her team "load mixed" to celebrate Christmas.

Now being a princess, Rapunzel had a lot of work to do. She was called for every occasion for example, Halloween, Christmas, Diwali, Eid, Orientation Day for new students and old students and for the graduation (there are also more occasions than just listed, the listed ones are the main ones). So you know she is packed the whole day. She has one more special power, she can die at any time of her time but she wishes to die when she has distributed her possessions between her children. This power is given to her by the crown. And so days pass by and the year 2026 ended and a new year starts which is 2027. This was the year when our pop princess was crowned as the Queen of Pop. The tradition is that if the king/queen of pop dies then the pop princess or the prince of pop becomes the king/queen of pop. And that time Jimmy, unfortunately, had died. That's a complete mystery how he died, even to his family. Rapunzel fell in love and got married on 8th September, 2027. During her marriage reception, Rapunzel sings a song for her husband written for her solo album by Jimmy before he died.

He dreamed that one day his daughter would sing it for her husband and fans which indeed became a reality.

A few months later,8th November 2028 on 8 Rapunzel was blessed with a son who is a working man in a company of his own. His name is kept after his grandfather, Jimmy Jackson. Unfortunately, Rapunzel had to leave her son under his father's care and go for recording studios and filming studios to sing and make videos for her songs. Just like MC Mary Kom, India's renowned Boxer. Years pass by, now this is the year 2070, and our queen of pop has 2 children, Jimmy, her elder son, and Sophia, her young daughter born on 11th December, 2039.

She lives her life in peace. And recently Published her autobiography named "the crowns". You might be thinking, how do I know her personal and professional life if I was and am her friend but still alive? Well, I was crowned the Lady Royal of Queen Rapunzel Jackson and still am. Women in our family have been Lady Royals to the princesses and the queens and to the wives of the kings. And we still are going to be.

#####

Together, Forever!!

-Nidhi & kanishka

Life a simple word though pretty difficult to lead without the loved ones. We love, we share and, we care and laugh out loud at times when we have no option left, we think for those who matter, but life would always be incomplete without the touch of feelings in it. Feelings that are always unconditional, true and make one feel belonged to. It was the auspicious day of dusshera , a festival that we Indians celebrate with all our devotion. It's been said that on this day Lord Rama (Symbol of Justice and truth) won the battle against Ravana(Symbol of evil). Manvi was very happy as she was pregnant and she firmly believed in God. She was blessed with a charm that only a woman is blessed with during her pregnancy. The charm brought a magical shine on her face that showed that she was contented, happy though emotional. She was in a phase where just a week was left from the date given by the doctor. She woke up early that day and with her wet hair left loose, a red traditional saree adorning her she was all ready to go for her 'pooja' preparations.

Manvi: Janvi(called her name to call her), come let's start the decoration . Janvi: Just a minute bhabhi, coming in a while.

Manvi: Okay dear, am waiting! As Janvi came out of her room: "Paay Lagu Bhabhi", bless me with your blessings!

(Janvi was a modern woman who was smart, educated, and working. But she also knew the importance of relationships and the way bonds can be tied smoothly) Manvi(Smiling Innocently): "Dudo Nahao, Puto Phalo" my little sister (May God bless you with health and lovely children). Janvi : Bhabhi you take a chair and command me. You should not stress out in this situation. You just guide me and I will look after all the preparations. After a while Janvi was done with all the preparations and she called rest of the family members which included her in-laws (Her husband's parents, chachaji and chachiji and their children). They all stayed as a joint family and respected each other. The family members gathered and appreciated both the daughter in laws for the preparations they have done. Manvi was very happy that day but destiny has its own plan. Manvi was going back to her room and a life taking accident occurred. An accident that was about to change everyone's life. The family that was laughing together a moment before was now in shock. Manvi's life was in danger, the baby was in danger. Manvi missed a step and slipped down from the staircase. Immediately Manvi was shifted to the hospital where she delivered a healthy baby. But the accident lead to the brain injury and Manvi was leading a life where she could only hear and sense, but couldn't speak or even caress her new born baby. The family was in dilemma. The new born baby needed the warmth of her mother.

Destiny always has a better plan and we can just act accordingly and do nothing!! Life looks like a rollercoaster ride when destiny slaps you from one end, and surprises you from the other side!!The dawn rises to spread light and sprinkles the dew drop as a gift to mankind, as if smiling and saying that God has blessed us with a new morning, get up and lead your life!!

It's been twenty long years and Nimit is now a young child. He is in the first year of the college and undergoing his engineering studies. A very famous and intellectual guy of his college, His physique looks like a sportsman (broad shoulder, slim waist) and a face that holds a heart taking smile. Today on his birthday he is being awarded with a champion trophy that he and his football team has won for the college in the inter college competition. At home everyone has planned a surprise party for him to celebrate his birthday and victory. "Mummaaa, Mumaa where are you? Am back home mumma! I did it again! Our team won the champion!"

I knew that. My son is the best among all. Love you beta said Janvi.

Nimit: Where is Manvi aunty? I want to show her my trophy and get her blessings. Janvi : She is in her room. I just gave her the medicine so that she can sleep and take rest.

Nimit: I'll just have a glance of her and come back, would surely not disturb her sleep. She is my inspiration who makes me win the battle every day, be it studies or football. I feel so relaxed in her company. She does not speak but her presence is enough for me. She is no less than a mother to me(with a thought of satisfaction) Janvi smiled at him and got engrossed in her work. *Life seems perfect by the time it does not start revealing the truth. The aura of truth can be sensed but can only be realized at a given and decided time.*

103

"I am back home" said Mr. Mihir.

" Go and change I am coming with tea. "Said Janvi.

" Beta tell your mom that kindly make tea for me too "(Another voice came of Mr. Tarun)

" Jee tayaji " Aarav said.

Mihir was Janvi's husband and Tarun was Manvi's husband. Aarav was Janvi's son.

" Bhaiya, tea ", Janvi said.

" Thanks Janvi " , Tarun said.

Janvi passed a fake smile.

" Beta, Are you sad ? " Tarun asked seeing Janvi's face.

" Nothing bhaiya " Janvi said.

" Did Nimit do anything" ? He asked again.

" No bhaiya I am actually worried for Nimit. "Janvi said.

" Can I know the reason? "Mihir came from behind.

"Lock the door " Janvi said. " Actually today his team won the trophy..... "Janvi had not completed her sentence and Mihir said " That's a wonderful news. I must go and congratulate him. "

" Chote, wait let Janvi complete her talk." Tarun said.

" Yes, he was very happy when he returned back. He said he wanted to show his trophy to his Manvi Aunty as she is his inspiration who makes him win the battle every day, be it studies or football. He feels so relaxed in her company. She does not speak but her presence is enough for him. She is no less than a mother to him. "Completed Janvi.

" And you are worried because he said Manvi is no less than a mother to him ?" Tarun asked.

" No bhaiya, Manvi bhabhi is Nimit's real mother. I am worried because he does not know this fact and how will he react when he will know the actual fact of his life. " Janvi completed with tears in her eyes.

" How will he know ? " Mihir asked.

" Today Aarav came to me in afternoon, he was telling that he heard society ladies talking that he is Janvi's real son. I told him that you misunderstood them as they were saying you're the real hero and Nimit bhaiya is called Superboy but you both know Aarav is not a kid anymore. He is 17 years young boy who we cannot fool for a long time and I am worried as today Aarav heard this but what if Nimit would have heard what would have happened?! " Janvi said.

" This is a serious issue " Mihir said.

" I have decided something " , Janvi said. " What ? " , Mihir asked.

" We must leave this place and shift to some other place where this secret remains a secret only. " Janvi said.

Mr. Tarun was silent.

" Bhaiya what do you think? Whatever you will say we will agree. Why are you silent? " Mihir being worried asked so many questions in a go.

"We are blessed to have Janvi in our family. If we go far away from this place Janvi will be at loss. She needs to quit her job. But for Janvi Nimit is more important than her job. " Tarun said.

"Oh bhaiya it's ok. " Janvi said.

"We will tell Nimit the truth " ,Tarun said.

"What?" Mihir and Janvi said together. "Yes, if he comes to know about this truth by someone else he will be very upset but if we will tell him, maybe he won't react much. The truth is to be revealed someday" were the words of Tarun.

"I am very scared." Janvi said.

* Knock knock *

"Ssshh wipe your tears", Mihir said and went to open the door.

"Aarav beta, come inside " Tarun said. "All three of you hid such a big thing from me. I never expected this. " Aarav shouted.

"Beta, please don't get angry , we were about to tell you " Mihir consoled.

"No, you are lying, if you wanted to tell me then before locking this door you would have called me too. " Mihir said.

"I guess you forgot that when elders talk children are not allowed. " Janvi said.

" I do remember mumma but you know Nimit bhaiya's birthday is so important and you all planned it without me. " Aarav said. By hearing this there was a sign of relief on all the three faces.

"Come we will plan with you!"Tarun said. "You all plan, I am going to see menu and inviting people ", Janvi said and left the room. If love of the mother could be defined the relation would not stand so important in everyone's life. It is not just a word or a tag given to a person just because of the birth, it's the bond one shares from the depth of the soul. Janvi was also a mother. She loved Nimit, and never had a sense of difference between Aarav and him.

Nimit (At the birthday bash) : " Mumma where is the special gift you have brought for me? "

Janvi:" Yes, the gift is actually very special. But I need a promise in turn that you will understand what I have to say. The gift is the truth of your life."

Nimit:" I promise. "

Janvi: " What if I say, I am not your mother? "

Nimit: "What do you mean by that?"

Janvi(heavy heartedly) : "Yes, I am not your real mother. Manvi bhabhi is your mother. I never told you as for me you are my elder son and would always be (with tears in her eyes)".

Nimit: " So? "

Janvi: Couldn't understand. (With a blank look)

Nimit: "You are and you would be my mumma always. I knew the truth before. I never revealed it as it never mattered to me. Manvi mumma has given birth to me, but you taught me the lessons of life. You are the one who taught me and made me the one I am today. I am a blessed child with two mothers. What else would I need after this? "

Janvi: "Are you angry on me? "

Nimit: "No mumma! How could I forget the values inculcated by you? You taught me to respect the elders. You taught me to live, laugh, share and care. You are the best thing that has happened to me. You are an angel for me. Just getting birth from a different mother would never detach me from you. Love given by you was never less, than how would I differentiate between you and Manvi mumma."

Janvi: "Sorry my child. I was scared to lose you. Everyone around used to criticize me, but now I am blessed enough to have a son like you. "

Janvi and Nimit hugged each other. For Janvi and Nimit the time rested there itself. It was a time to celebrate in real sense. (The party begun and they all celebrated with all the charm and happiness they had) Family is a place where you grow as a human. Your upbringing defines you, and the same was true for Nimit.

True relations are always undefined, let them remain undefined!

#####